"I can help you."

"For a price," she said bitterly. "Well, it's too high to pay. I won't—"

He pulled her close against him and kissed her. She fought him and he clasped her face between his hands, held her still, held her mouth to his until he felt her start to tremble.

"Marry me," he said in a husky whisper, "and your grandmother's life will go on as it always has."

"That's blackmail!"

"It's a simple statement of fact."

"I won't sell myself to you."

"Is that how you see an arranged marriage that will benefit two families? How many del Vecchio brides have been 'sold' over the centuries, do you think?"

"My grandmother wouldn't do this for money."

"For money. For the del Vecchio name to remain powerful. For an infusion of new blood." His eyes grew hot. "She wants an heir. So do I."

Sandra Marton is an author who used to tell stories to her dolls when she was a little girl. Today, readers around the world fall in love with her sexy, dynamic heroes and outspoken, independent heroines. Her books have topped bestseller lists and won many awards. Sandra loves dressing up for a night out with her husband as much as she loves putting on her hiking boots for a walk in a desert or a forest. You can write to her (SASE) at PO Box 295, Storrs, Connecticut, USA, or e-mail her at www.sandramarton.com

Recent titles by the same author:

The Barons:
MARRIAGE ON THE EDGE
MORE THAN A MISTRESS
SLADE BARON'S BRIDE
THE TAMING OF TYLER KINCAID
MISTRESS OF THE SHEIKH
THE ALVARES BRIDE
THE PREGNANT MISTRESS
RAISING THE STAKES (Mills & Boon® Single Title)

The O'Connells:
KEIR O'CONNELL'S MISTRESS

THE BORGHESE BRIDE

BY
SANDRA MARTON

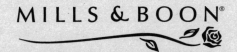

MILLS & BOON and MILLS & BOON with the Rose Device are registered trademarks of the publisher.

First published in Great Britain 2003
Harlequin Mills & Boon Limited,
Eton House, 18-24 Paradise Road, Richmond, Surrey TW9 1SR

© Sandra Myles 2003

ISBN 0 263 83247 3

Set in Times Roman 10½ on 11¼ pt.
01-0703-48799

Printed and bound in Spain
by Litografía Rosés, S.A., Barcelona

CHAPTER ONE

ITALY was in the midst of the hottest summer anyone could recall. This last week in July, people said, would go down in the records.

For Dominic Borghese, the last week in July was already memorable. It had been for the last five years.

Dominic took a pair of dark glasses from the visor in his cherry-red Ferrari and slipped them on as he sped along a narrow road in the Tuscan hills.

He'd made errors in his life. He'd never been too proud to admit that. A man didn't rise from the gutter as Dominic had without making an occasional misjudgment, but the memory and the scale of the errors he'd made that last week in July five long years ago stayed with him.

One involved a loan he never should have made.

The other involved a woman.

Of the two mistakes, the loan was easiest to write off. In fact, he was on his way to do that this morning. It had bothered him for years that he'd agreed to the loan in the first place. Not the money, but the terms he'd accepted.

Dominic had no wish whatsoever to acquire ownership of the company the *Marchesa* del Vecchio had put up as collateral. She was an old woman; he'd accepted her offer rather than simply given her the amount she'd requested because he'd known her pride would not let her take the money otherwise.

Now, thanks to his accountants and some discreet inquiries, he knew she would not be able to pay the debt. Well, he'd find a way to tell her he was wiping the slate clean when he saw her in less than an hour. If that wounded her precious, blue-blooded pride, so be it.

Dominic stepped down on the gas pedal.

The other mistake, which he'd made at the start of that same week five years before, was impossible to rectify.

He'd been in New York on business, attended a charity function that bored him out of his skull, gone out on the terrace to get away from the idle chatter, the flashbulbs, the women coming on to him with faces made perfect by injections and nips and tucks and God only knew what...

And found himself in his apartment less than an hour later, making love to a nameless woman with a beautiful face, a soft voice and a desire as quick and hot as his...a woman who'd slipped from his bed while he slept.

He'd never seen her again.

And he'd never forgotten her.

Dominic's jaw tightened.

It was stupid to still think about her, but he knew the reason. She'd been a mystery that night, a blond, blue-eyed vision in a white silk suit, refusing to give him her name, saying as he took her in his arms that this was all a dream and that it must stay that way.

How could a man forget a mystery?

He could still remember the taste of her mouth, the scent of her skin, the feel of her body under his hands.

Stupid, indeed. If only he could expunge the memory of the woman as easily as he was going to expunge the debt of the *marchesa*...

Dominic sighed.

For a man who'd begun life with the deck stacked against him, these odds really weren't bad. One out of two. Surely, he could live with that.

He relaxed a little, shifting his long legs under the dashboard, loosening his grip on the leather-covered steering wheel. There was no point in even thinking about the woman. Thinking about the *marchesa* was different. He'd be at her *palazzo* in half an hour and he still hadn't come up with an easy way to tell her he didn't want her money;

not the principal, not the interest, and most assuredly not the company she'd put up as collateral.

Thinking about it made him smile. If those he did business with knew what he was planning, they'd never believe it.

At thirty-four, Dominic owned the world, or so people said. Men who'd come up the hard way, as he had, admired him. Men who had inherited their wealth instead of wresting their first million from a sweltering emerald pit in a Brazilian jungle, smiled to his face and slandered him behind his back. Dominic knew it but didn't give a damn. Only a fool would judge a man by the blueness of his blood.

So what if they could trace their ancestry back through the centuries? He could trace his to an alcoholic mother who'd chosen his surname because she guessed he'd been conceived one dark night near the walls of the Villa Borghese.

At twelve, the sordid little story had been painful to hear. By thirty, just about the time he realized he'd already earned more money than most of his detractors would make in a lifetime, it had lost its bite.

The most recent rumor said that he was descended from an illicit liaison between a sixteenth-century Roman prince and a housemaid.

Dominic found it amusing.

Gossip couldn't touch his wealth or his power, and it certainly didn't keep women from his bed.

They were always stunning, their faces often familiar to readers of society and celebrity columns. They were women with good minds—dull ones bored him—and invariably they had careers and pursuits of their own. Dominic preferred it that way because he had no wish for commitment. Not yet. Thirty-five had always seemed the right age to find a wife who would look good on his arm, make sure his home was a quiet, comfortable haven, and give him an heir.

A son would truly make the name Borghese legitimate.

Wealth, power, legitimacy. What more could one ask from the bastard son of a street-walker?

But not just yet.

He had a year to go before he turned thirty-five. Until then, he was going to go on enjoying his freedom…and occasionally toy with the idea of having his people locate the woman from that hot July night in New York. He'd almost done it five years ago, but why give a simple sexual encounter more importance than it deserved? Just because he couldn't get her out of his mind…

"Hell," Dominic muttered, and floored the gas pedal.

Concentrate, he told himself. Concentrate on the task that lay ahead. Perhaps if he reviewed that first encounter with the *marchesa,* he'd find a hint in it of how he could tell her to keep the three million American dollars he'd lent her and keep her pride as well.

It was a significant sum of money and he wasn't a bank, which was precisely what he'd told the lady the day she'd come to see him at his office.

Come to see him? That was putting a spin on it. The *marchesa* had invaded his office. She was eighty years old and frail-looking, but she'd managed to bully her way past the information desk in the lobby, past the receptionist on the floor that belonged only to him, and almost past his secretary.

Nobody, not even the *Marchesa* del Vecchio, could get by Celia.

"There's a woman insisting on seeing you," Celia had told him and when Dominic sighed, she'd put her hands on her hips and said no, not *that* woman—he'd been in the process of politely easing himself out of a relationship that had gone stale. This woman, Celia had said, was elderly. She had a sharp tongue and a short temper.

Dominic had lifted one dark eyebrow. "Do I know her?"

"She says you met at the opera. She is the *Marchesa* del Vecchio."

"I don't recall."

Celia told him the rest, that the *marchesa* had somehow talked her way past both the desk and the reception area.

"Really." Dominic's green eyes narrowed. "Tell the people at both desks that if such a thing happens again, they're fired. And tell the *marchesa* I'll see her. Five minutes, Celia. That's all. After that—"

"Ring your private line. Yes. I know."

He stood in the doorway to greet his uninvited guest. She was a slender, white-haired woman with a ramrod-straight posture that had probably been bred into her elegant bones, though now she needed an ebony walking stick to maintain it.

"*Marchesa*. What a delightful surprise."

"Nonsense. I am sure that my visit is a surprise, Signore Borghese, but I am not so foolish to think it is a delightful one. Why would a handsome young man like you be happy to see an old woman like me?"

She was forthright. Dominic liked that. Few people were when dealing with him. He helped her to a chair across from his desk and sat down.

"May I offer you some tea?"

"It is four in the afternoon, *signore*. Do you generally take tea at this hour?"

"Well, no. To be honest—"

"I have heard you are always honest. It is the reason I am here." The *marchesa* rapped her stick sharply against the terrazzo floor. "Sherry," she barked at Celia, hovering in the doorway. "Very dry."

Dominic glanced at his secretary. "For both of us, *prego*," he said smoothly and tried to make small talk with his visitor, who clearly had no interest in accommodating him. He breathed a small sigh of relief when, at last, they were alone with a silver tray bearing two small glasses and a decanter on the table between then. *"Marchesa,"* he said, lifting his glass.

The *marchesa* nodded, took a delicate sip of sherry and got down to business.

She told him something all Italy had known for some four hundred years. The del Vecchio money came from land holdings outside Florence and from a family-owned business called *La Farfalla di Seta.* The business had been started in the fifteenth century by the third *Marchesa* del Vecchio, whose husband had gambled away his fortune and left her penniless. That *marchesa* and her daughters, schooled in the delicate arts of sewing and embroidery as ladies were in those days, fed herself and her household by making lingerie of fine silk and lace. It was hand-stitched, hand-embroidered, and handsomely priced.

It was very expensive still. Dominic knew from personal experience. Lingerie from *La Farfalla di Seta* was a gift much appreciated by beautiful women.

"I have heard of it," he said politely.

"The Silk Butterfly," the *marchesa* said with distaste. "That is how it is known in America, where our business is now located. I do not like that name. We are an old and honorable family enterprise with our roots, our heart, in *Firenze.* In Florence," she'd added, as if Dominic might not understand the language of his birth. "But I am not a fool, *signore.* I know that it is American taste that leads the way. Like it or not, those who expect to succeed must follow."

"Please, call me Dominic. And tell me why you've come here, *Marchesa.*"

The old woman didn't bother offering courtesy for courtesy by suggesting he dispose with her title. Instead, she put down her glass and folded both gnarled hands around the silver head of her walking stick.

"The Silk Butterfly is my most prized possession."

"And?"

"And, I need six billion *lire.*"

"Three million U.S. dollars?" Dominic blinked. "I beg your pardon?"

"My granddaughter is in charge of our operation. She tells me we face competition. She tells me we are in desperate need of modernizing, that we must move from where we have been for fifty years to a different location. She tells me—"

"She tells you a great deal," Dominic said with some amusement, "this granddaughter of yours. Are you sure she is right?"

"I am not here for advice, *signore.*"

"Dominic."

"Nor am I here so you can question my granddaughter's decisions. She has been in charge of *La Farfalla* for several years. More importantly, I raised her after the death of her parents. She is Italian enough to understand the importance of the company to our *famiglia,* but American enough to understand the importance of staying in business, which we will not do without an infusion of capital. That is why I have come to you, *signore,* as I said. I need six billion *lire.*"

Dominic's private telephone line rang. Celia, he thought, and not a moment too soon.

"I see," he said, reaching for the phone. He put his palm over the mouthpiece and smiled politely. "Well, I wish I could help you, *Marchesa,* but I am not a bank. And, as I'm sure you realize, my time—"

"—is valuable," the old woman snapped. "As is mine."

"Of course. Forgive me, but this call—"

"The call is from the watchdog who guards your door. Tell her I am not yet done, *signore,* and I shall do my best to take no more than five more minutes of your precious morning."

Dominic couldn't recall the last time someone had spoken to him that way. Those who came to him for a favor shuffled their feet, at least metaphorically. The *marchesa* was an irritant, an annoyance…and a breath of fresh air.

He put the phone to his ear, told Celia to hold his calls, then steepled his hands under his chin.

"Why would you come to me for money, *Marchesa?* As I said, I am not a bank."

Her answer was blunt. "I have been to the banks. They turned me down."

"Because?"

"Because they are foolish enough to think a small company cannot succeed, because they think the days when women were willing to spend hundreds of dollars for a frivolous garment are over, because they believe my granddaughter should not bear the entire responsibility for The Silk Butterfly."

"And you think they're wrong?"

"I know they are," the *marchesa* said impatiently. "Women will always covet expensive nonsense and if they don't buy it themselves, men will buy it for them."

"What about your granddaughter? Are you so sure she's capable of running The Silk Butterfly?"

If a woman like the *marchesa* could be said to snort, that was what she did.

"My granddaughter has a degree in business from an American university. She is smart, determined, and capable of doing anything she sets her mind to. She is like me."

Dominic nodded. He had no doubt that was true. He could easily envision a middle-aged duplicate of the old woman seated opposite him, a sharp-tongued spinster with a stern expression and a no-nonsense attitude.

"All right," he said. "You want me to lend you money. Tell me why I should."

"Borghese International recently acquired a French fashion group."

Dominic was impressed. The news of the financial coup had not yet become public knowledge.

"And?"

"And," the *marchesa* said impatiently, "surely you can see the benefits of incorporating our name and clientele under the one umbrella."

Dominic sat back. There might be some benefit, yes. He could get an answer from his research team, but he doubted it would be worth three million dollars. And why would the *marchesa* tell him the importance of *La Farfalla* to her family and then offer to sell it to him?

"Let me understand this, *Marchesa*. You are asking me to buy—"

"I am asking you to lend me money, young man. How many times must I repeat myself? You will make the loan, I will agree to repay it in five years at a rate of interest upon which we will agree."

"So, you don't wish to sell to me?"

"Are you deaf? No. I do not wish to sell to you or anyone else. I speak of a loan. Only a loan."

Puzzled, Dominic shook his head. "I repeat, *Marchesa*, I am not a bank."

For the first time since she'd entered his office, the *marchesa* seemed to hesitate.

"I am willing to admit there is some small risk in what I ask."

"And?"

"And, for the courtesy of making me the loan, I will give you a five percent interest in The Silk Butterfly."

Dominic said nothing. Five percent of a failing company was a pathetic offer, but he was too polite to tell her that.

"Should I not be able to repay you…" The *marchesa* drew a deep breath. "Should such an unlikely thing happen, you will become the sole owner of *La Farfalla di Seta*. And your French fashion group will be able to make their own garments using that name."

The old woman sat back, hands still folded around the walking stick, but now Dominic saw that her hands trembled. For the first time he realized what it had taken to bring her here. She had to be in desperate financial straits. She'd probably pledged all her assets to keep the company going, but what she was putting on the line now were her family's name and heritage—her most valuable possessions.

His people would confirm tomorrow what he was sure he knew today. The *marchesa* was broke and in debt up to her eyeballs, and what she was offering in return for three million dollars was probably not worth half that amount to him. He knew he should tell her that but for a man who was reputed to have no heart, he couldn't bring himself to do it quite so directly.

"I have heard that you are a man willing to gamble," she'd said, while he searched for words. "Is that not the way you began your fortune, Signore Borghese? By risking everything, including your very life, on a project that was dangerous and even foolhardy?" She smiled and he glimpsed the girl she must once have been. "You stand to lose nothing, Dominic. It is I who must take the risk this time, not you."

At that, Dominic had risen from his chair and gently drawn the old woman to her feet.

"Done," he'd said. "Three million American dollars, five years to repay at two percent."

"Eight and a half."

He'd laughed. "Does a bargain offend you, *Marchesa?*"

"Charity offends me when it is not needed. Eight and a half percent, *signore*. That is, as they say, the going rate."

"Four."

"Six and a half, and that is my final offer."

Dominic thought about reminding her that it wasn't the borrower who made offers, it was the lender. Instead, he'd lifted her hand to his lips.

"You drive a hard bargain, *Marchesa*. Very well. Six and a half percent, repayable in five years."

"And five percent of The Silk Butterfly will be yours as soon as the papers are drawn up."

"*Marchesa,* that really isn't…" The look on her face had stopped him. "Fine. Let your attorney send me the papers to sign and I… What's the matter?"

"I prefer not to have my attorney do this, *signore.* If you could deal with the legal aspects…?"

He knew what that meant. Her attorney would tell her she was making a bad deal. Dominic sighed. His would tell him the same thing.

"*Marchesa,*" he'd said gently, "perhaps we could simply pledge our honor on our deal, yes?"

The old woman had smiled and placed her hand in his, and he had not seen or heard from her until yesterday when she'd called his office and invited him to lunch at her *palazzo.* He'd almost declined, but then he'd recalled the report that had confirmed his suspicion that she couldn't possibly pay off the loan that was now due in less than three days, and he'd said he'd be delighted.

Ahead, tall iron gates stretched across the narrow road. He'd reached the *palazzo* and he still hadn't come up with a way to leave the *marchesa* her pride while telling her he was writing off the loan.

Dominic slowed the Ferrari, looked up at a camera mounted in a tall cypress and waited as the gate slid open.

Perhaps he could tell her a complex tale of taxes, of the benefits to her and to him if she would permit him to declare the money he'd lent her a bad debt.

It just might work.

An hour later, over *espresso* served in sixteenth-century *cristallo* cups, he knew that his scheme was doomed. The *marchesa* had politely avoided talk of business until they'd finished eating. Now, at the first reference to taxes, profits and losses, she waved her hand in dismissal.

"Let us spare each other polite chitchat and get to the

truth, *signore*. As you probably already suspect, I cannot repay the money I owe you.''

Dominic nodded. "I did suspect that, yes. But it's not a problem."

"No, it is not. We have an agreement. The Silk Butterfly is yours."

Her head was high but the quaver in her voice gave her away. Dominic sighed in exasperation.

"*Marchesa*. Please listen to me. I cannot—"

"You can. You must. That was our agreement."

Dominic ran a hand through his hair. "Agreements can be changed."

"Not for people of honor," she said coldly, "which we both are."

"We are, yes, but...I wish to forgive you the money, *Marchesa*. Truly, I don't need it. I give more to charity each—" A mistake. He knew it as soon as he said it. "I didn't mean—"

"The del Vecchios do not accept charity."

"No. Certainly not. I simply wanted to—"

"You wanted to renege on the terms of our arrangement."

"No. Yes. Dammit, *Marchesa*..."

"It is not necessary to resort to profanity, Signore Borghese."

Dominic shot to his feet. "I am not resorting to anything but logic. Surely you can see that."

The *marchesa* lifted her head. Her eyes, still a vibrant blue, pinned him mercilessly to the spot. Such a vibrant blue, Dominic thought, frowning. Where had he seen that color before?

"What I see," she said, "is that I misjudged you. I thought you were a person of honor."

Dominic stiffened. "If you were a man," he said softly, "you would never get away with saying something like that to me."

"Then do not try to avoid complying with our agreement."

Dominic stared at the haughty old face, mumbled a word learned on the streets in his childhood under his breath, and paced across the dining room. He covered the distance from one wall to the other three times before turning toward the *marchesa* again.

"I would not be a man of honor if I took The Silk Butterfly from you. You may not see it that way, but that's how it is."

The *marchesa* sighed. "I suppose I can see your point."

Later, Dominic would realize she'd agreed far too quickly but at that moment, all he felt was relief.

"I will agree to a change in terms."

"Excellent." Dominic reached for the old woman's hand. "And now, if you will forgive me, it's a long drive back to—"

"You must admit," the *marchesa* said softly, "The Silk Butterfly would make an excellent addition to your French fashion group."

Something in her tone gave him pause, but he knew her pride made it necessary for her to hear him say she was right.

"Yes. Yes, I agree, it probably would have. But—"

The old woman rapped her cane against the floor, as she had in Dominic's office five years before. A maid appeared, so quickly it was apparent she'd been waiting in the hall, hurried toward them and handed the *marchesa* a silver picture frame.

"During this entire time," the *marchesa* said, as she waved the maid out, "did you never think to meet my granddaughter?"

"Why would I? You told me she was more than capable of running The Silk Butterfly."

"She is." The *marchesa* looked at the photo she held in her hands and smiled. "Still, I'd hoped you and Arianna would have become acquainted.'' Her eyes lifted to his. ''She is a woman you would find appealing, I am sure.''

Dio, was that where this was leading? Was this the price of the old woman's pride? Dominic had spent more than any man's fair share of evenings listening politely to what could only be described as sales pitches on the fine qualities of young women whose families found his money sufficient reason to overcome any qualms they might have about his lineage. Was he going to have to endure an hour's worth of paeans about the *marchesa's* spinster granddaughter? Her unattractive, overaged, undersexed…

The *marchesa* turned the picture toward him. Dominic felt the blood drain from his head. He was looking at a face he'd seen before, a face that still haunted his dreams after five years. Hair the color of sunlight. Elegant cheekbones. A soft pink mouth and eyes a shade of blue he suddenly recognized, for he'd seen them in the face of the *marchesa.*

Somehow, he managed to draw air into his lungs.

''Who is this?''

''My granddaughter, of course. Arianna.''

Arianna. The name suited the woman. Dominic's head was spinning. He needed air.

''*Marchesa.* I think—I really think…'' He cleared his throat. ''I must leave. It's getting late and the drive back to Rome is—''

''Long. Of course. But surely you want to hear the way in which I propose to settle our debt.''

''Not now. Another time. Tomorrow, or the next day, but—''

''But what? My Arianna is beautiful. Surely you can see that.''

''She is, yes. But—''

''She is bright and healthy and of child-bearing age.''

''What?'' Dominic barked out a laugh. ''*Marchesa.* For heaven's sake—''

''You are not getting any younger. Neither is she. Don't

you want to breed sons? Don't you want to found a dy-
nasty?'' The *marchesa* raised her chin. ''Or continue one
as old as mine and Arianna's?''

Dominic dragged in another breath. ''Surely you aren't
suggesting—''

''Surely I am. Marry my granddaughter, Signore Borghese. Merge our two houses. You will gain The Silk Butterfly and I will not lose it. Then we will both know that
the del Vecchio debt is fully paid.''

CHAPTER TWO

IT WAS a perfect summer morning in New York. Not too hot, not too humid. Just perfect.

Perfect, except for The Silk Butterfly.

Arianna del Vecchio Cabot, seated in an eighteenth-century chair that was her legacy through her father's family, the Mayflower Cabots, her elbows resting on a fifteenth-century desk that was her legacy through her mother's family, the del Vecchios of Florence, sighed and looked out the window of her office.

In a city of offices filled with computers, Arianna's place of work appeared to be an anachronism.

It was an expensive, deliberate illusion.

The Silk Butterfly was housed in a modern building on a busy street, but once you stepped past the front door, you found yourself in a replica of a Florentine *palazzo*. High ceilings, frescoed walls, travertine marble floors and soft lighting all combined to suggest an earlier, more gracious time.

The *New York Times* had done a piece on the Butterfly's new look and location four years earlier and dubbed it "elegant." *A LA MODE* magazine had shown less restraint by pronouncing the place sexy and exciting. It was, said a TV entertainment program, the ultimate in romantic settings.

Yes! Arianna had thought when she'd heard those descriptions. Moving had been a big, incredibly expensive gamble but hearing such accolades had convinced her she'd done the right thing. Until then, the Butterfly's primary customers had been old-line society matrons who'd bought their trousseaus at the shop half a century before. Arianna wanted to hold on to them but she also wanted to appeal to young women with the taste and money to indulge in the sexy lingerie her new design team created.

The Silk Butterfly had been a diamond mounted in a Victorian setting instead of a Tiffany solitaire, its beauty recognized by only a select few.

The action, as the fashion magazines called it, had all moved out of the old neighborhood. Arianna had known they had to move with it, but first she'd had to convince her grandmother. Then she'd had to wait for the necessary capital, find the right location, the right architect and builder.

The result was breathtaking. Young women with high-powered jobs flocked to the Butterfly. So did the men who were their lovers.

There was only one catch. By the time Arianna opened the new shop, it was too late. Dot-coms failed. Technology stocks crumpled. Men who'd thought nothing of buying a few thousand dollars worth of silk for the women they wanted to impress were jobless. Women who'd splurged on sexy lace to wear under their serious wool suits went back to wearing garments bought off the rack.

The Silk Butterfly was still beautiful, still a place that made people ooh and aah. Unfortunately, they oohed and aahed without spending money. The old clients, ladies with white hair and financial managers far too conservative to have succumbed to the allure of the internet, could still afford the Butterfly's luxuries, but they didn't buy the outrageously expensive new designs. And when the tenor of the times made people turn away from frivolity, the eventual default of the loan her grandmother had taken became a certainty. The Butterfly was doomed. A family-owned business that had flourished for centuries was about to die. Arianna lived each day knowing it was she who'd delivered the fatal wound.

How much longer until her small kingdom was gone? The loan was due tomorrow, but the dissolution of a complex business took time. Bankers, accountants, attorneys would gather to pick over the corpse. Like the captain of a ship, she'd be expected to remain on board until it went under.

Arianna gave another deep sigh. It was one hell of a badly mixed metaphor, but it summed things up. The Butterfly was dying and she would have to watch it happen.

The worst part had been telling her grandmother. She'd written her a long letter and detailed all the steps she'd taken to try and save the business. The *marchesa* had responded with a note that said Arianna was not to blame herself.

"You have done all you possibly could," the old woman had assured her.

Arianna rose and walked slowly to the ornate indoor balcony just outside her office and looked down on the sales floor. Such a big, beautiful space. So handsomely designed, with lace and silk nightgowns and teddies and thongs artfully displayed.

And so empty.

Nobody was in the Butterfly except the one salesclerk she'd kept on until the closing.

Maybe the *marchesa* was right. Maybe she'd done all she could, but that didn't keep her from feeling guilty.

Almost five years ago, her grandmother had put three million dollars into the Butterfly. Without the money, they'd probably have gone under back then. Now, the business wouldn't just go under, it would be transformed from a place of tasteful intimacy to an unidentifiable cog in a giant money machine.

The Silk Butterfly was about to fall into the hands of a man named Dominic Borghese.

Arianna had never met him, but she knew all about him. Borghese was ruthless. Heartless. He flaunted his wealth and power. He'd come up from the mean streets of Rome and he never let anyone forget it.

The only bright spot in what was happening—if you could call it that—was that the loss of the business would not touch her grandmother's personal accounts. The *marchesa* would lose the Butterfly but not any of her own fortune.

She'd assured Arianna of that.

"They tell me it would not be prudent to invest my personal funds, Arianna," the old woman had explained. "That is why I've taken a loan."

And a good thing, too. Had her grandmother lost such a huge sum of money, the guilt would have been unbearable.

Arianna went back to her desk and took a small tin of aspirin from the top drawer.

Who could have dreamed things would end like this, when she'd first gone to work for the *marchesa* straight out of college?

"You are the future of *La Farfalla*," her grandmother had told her. "I want you to look ahead and recommend changes in how we do business."

Arianna had made recommendations but the *marchesa* vetoed them all. After six frustrating months, she'd left and gone to work for a fashion house. Sales at the Butterfly continued to fall while Arianna made a name for herself with her new employer.

A year passed. Then one morning the *marchesa* phoned. Arianna was to fly to Florence to meet with her at the *palazzo*. The matter was of some urgency. That was all she would say.

The meeting had been brief and to the point.

"I wish you to return to *La Farfalla di Seta*," the *marchesa* had said. "I am getting old, child. No, don't waste my time or yours in denial. I was wrong not taking your advice before. We need a young woman's energy and vision to lead us."

"I'm flattered, *Nonna*," Arianna had said with caution, "but the last time I was in charge of planning, you—"

"I'm not asking you to take charge of planning. I'm telling you that I am stepping aside. Don't look so surprised. Centuries of del Vecchio blood run in your veins."

"Cabot blood, too," Arianna had added. Despite having sent her to an American boarding school, her grandmother generally preferred to ignore that part of Arianna's lineage.

"That is another reason for you to take over. You understand the American market, and it generates the most profit. Clearly, you are the woman to lead us now."

And just look where she'd led it.

Arianna filled a Venetian glass tumbler with water from a carafe and gulped down three aspirin.

Maybe she shouldn't have made the move downtown. Maybe she should have made it sooner. Maybe she should have anticipated the economy's free fall.

Maybe she should give up second-guessing. What was done was done.

Hadn't she learned that lesson in a stranger's arms five years ago?

You couldn't travel the road ahead by looking back. She had to concentrate on what to do next, on how to support herself…

Herself, and her son.

Arianna drew a deep breath.

Her son.

She reached for the framed photo that was her desk's only ornamentation. A little boy looked out at the world from the silver frame, his eyes big and dark, his hair a tumble of black curls.

Jonathan del Vecchio Cabot. Her heart, her joy, her secret. Her child, fathered by a stranger.

It still seemed impossible.

One indiscretion. One night's passion in the arms of a man who didn't know her name any more than she knew his, and her life had changed forever.

She'd met him at a charity party at a hotel on Fifth Avenue. Met him? That wasn't what had happened. She hadn't "met" the man, she'd gone to bed with him.

How? How could she have done such a thing? Five long years had passed and she still had no answer.

She'd only gone to the party because she'd begun planning the Butterfly's expansion and high-powered parties were good places to make connections. Half an hour after stepping into the ballroom, she'd regretted the decision. The place was a sea of noise and glitter. Arianna was as adept at making small talk as anyone, but not that particular night.

She'd watched the expensively dressed women air-kissing the cheeks of other expensively dressed women, the men with them exchanging equally phony smiles and handshakes, and she'd longed for the simplicity and quiet of her apartment on Gramercy Park.

She'd been edging toward one of the terraces for a breath of fresh air when she saw the man. He was tall and dark-haired and almost dangerously beautiful. And he was watching her, his face taut with the hunger of a mountain lion as it watches its unwary prey.

Arianna felt her skin turn hot. She'd wanted to tear her eyes from his but she couldn't. Like a stricken doe, she'd stood absolutely still, half the length of the ballroom between them, while her heart pounded.

He knew what she was feeling, what he was doing to her. His eyes had narrowed and told her so. She'd felt her bones start to melt.

Go home, she'd told herself, *Arianna, for God's sake, get out of here while you can.*

Instead, she'd moved slowly toward him. When he held out his hand, she took it, felt the strength of him as his fingers claimed hers. She let him lead her out on the terrace and then she was in his arms, his mouth crushing hers, her arms winding around his neck, her body pressed shamelessly against his.

Arianna's hand shook. Carefully, she put down the picture.

She'd never felt anything like that excitement in her life. She'd had a couple of lovers. The relationships had been discreet. Pleasant. Dinner and the theater. A movie, a museum, walks in Central Park and, after a while, kisses and caresses and sex.

Nothing like that had happened with the stranger. There'd been no preliminaries. No pretense at anything more than hunger. They hadn't even exchanged names. They hadn't said much of anything but what needed to be said.

"You're exquisite," he'd whispered, his voice deep and brushed with an accent. "My Princess of the Night. And I want you more than I've ever wanted another woman."

He'd touched her then. While they stood on the terrace, where anyone could have come out and seen them. He'd cupped her face, taken her mouth with his, run his hands down her body and slipped them under her short skirt and—and God, oh God, she'd come apart.

"Come with me," he'd said.

And she'd gone. To his penthouse suite high atop the hotel. To his bed, where he'd made love to her, with her, where he'd done things that had made her peak again and again in his arms.

A soft sound burst from Arianna's throat. She shut her eyes, trying to close out the memories, but she hadn't been able to do that in five long years. The images were crystal-clear. The feel of his body against hers. The taste of his mouth. How she'd responded to him, so wild and hot and hungry for everything he gave, everything he took.

She remembered the shock of awareness when it was over, how she'd stared into the darkness, waited until his breathing slowed, how she'd eased from his bed, dressed in the dark, taxied to her apartment where she'd showered and showered until her skin felt raw, trying to forget what she'd done.

But forgetting was impossible.

A month later, she missed her period. She'd been late before; that was what she'd told herself even as she bought a pregnancy test kit at the drugstore. And the man she'd gone to bed with had used a condom. Condoms, she'd thought, her face heating as she remembered the night.

But condoms weren't one hundred percent reliable. And she wasn't late. She was pregnant. Pregnant, by a man whose name she didn't even know.

She'd handled it by pretending it wasn't happening, until she awoke one morning sick to her stomach. Forced to face reality, she'd made an appointment with her gynecologist.

"I can't have this baby," she'd told him.

But on the day of the scheduled procedure she'd looked at herself, naked, in her bathroom mirror. There was a life growing inside her still-flat belly.

Instead of keeping her appointment she'd driven to Connecticut and stopped at the first realtor's office she saw in a little town she'd passed through during a weekend in the country.

A month later, she'd signed the papers for a pretty little house three hours and a million lifetimes from Manhattan and anyone she knew. Step one, she'd thought, and girded herself for step two, telling the *marchesa* about her pregnancy—but her grandmother had suffered a heart attack before she had the chance. Her doctors were sure she'd recover fully but from now on, she'd have to take things a bit easier.

That had been the end of Arianna's news.

To this day, she'd never told the *marchesa* about her pregnancy, her baby's birth, her son's very existence.

Nobody knew.

Jonathan was Arianna's sweet secret. She spent weekdays at her city condo, weekends and vacations in the sunny country house where her child, and her heart, had taken up residence.

The stranger had stolen her self-respect, but he'd given her a son she adored.

Impulsively, she reached for the telephone and pressed a button. Jonathan's nanny answered. A moment later, Arianna heard her son's voice.

"Hello, Mommy."

"Hello, darling. Susan says you had a picnic under the big maple tree."

"Uh-huh. Susan made cupcakes with funny faces. An' she made hard-boiled eggs with faces, too. Olives for the eyes an' that red stuff for the mouths."

"Pimiento," Arianna said, and wished, as she did every day, that she could be in Connecticut instead of here. At least one good thing would come of the Butterfly's demise. She'd sell the condo, find a job closer to home, spend every day and night with her little boy.

"Mommy? Are you coming home tonight?"

Arianna swallowed hard. Her son always asked the same question.

"I can't, baby. But tomorrow is Friday, remember? I'll be home by supper time and we'll have the whole weekend together."

They talked for another few minutes. Arianna didn't want to end the call but Jonathan said, with childish innocence, that he had to go because Susan was going to take him on an adventure to find the lost wolf cave.

"Have fun," Arianna said cheerfully.

She hung up the phone, leaned her elbows on her desk and pressed her hands to her eyes. Ridiculous, this sting of tears. Susan loved Jonathan and he loved her. That was good, wasn't it? She didn't have to worry about him every day, she only had to miss him—

"Arianna?"

"Yes?" Arianna sat up straight and looked at her assistant, standing in the doorway. "What is it, Tom?"

"You okay?"

"I'm fine. Just a headache, that's all. What's happening?"

"Your grandmother's on line three. Your private line was busy, so—"

"Thanks." Arianna picked up the phone as Tom closed the door behind him. *"Nonna?"*

"Arianna," the voice at the other end said in familiar, imperious tones, "I have been trying to reach you for hours. How long can you possibly stay on the telephone?"

Arianna smiled. "It's nice to hear from you, grandmother. How are you feeling today?"

"Impatient. How else would I feel, waiting to talk with you, waiting for this dreadful Manhattan traffic to move?"

"I was on the phone, grand—" Arianna frowned. "Manhattan traffic?"

"Driver? How much longer until we reach SoNo?"

"SoHo," Arianna said automatically. "Are you in New York?"

"Certainly I'm in New York. Didn't you get my message? I telephoned your office yesterday"

Arianna riffled through the stack of papers on the side of her desk. "No. No, I didn't. Grandmother, you shouldn't have made this trip. You know what your doctors said."

"They said I'm fine and that I can do as I wish."

"I don't think—"

"Good. Don't think. Listen instead. We will be at your office in half an hour. That's what the driver says, though I suspect that will only be possible if this limousine sprouts wings."

"What limousine? And who is 'we?'"

Static crackled across the line. "I can't hear you, Arianna."

Arianna switched the telephone to her other ear. Was her

grandmother on a cell phone? It didn't seem possible. The *marchesa* distrusted things like cell phones and computers, and couldn't be convinced to use them.

"*Nonna?* Can you hear me?"

"I—" Crackle. "…barely hear…" Crackle. "…tea for me…" Crackle. "…coffee for Signore…" Crackle. "…soon, Arianna."

"Grandmother? Grandmother!"

The line went dead.

Arianna hung up the phone, frowned and pressed the intercom button. "Tom? Did my grandmother call yesterday? No. I didn't think she— No. Never mind. No problem. Just—would you put up some tea, please? Coffee, too, and a plate of chocolate *biscotti* would be fine."

Why was the *marchesa* in New York? Perhaps she'd decided to be present at the closing of The Silk Butterfly. And who was with her? Her lawyer? Her accountant?

Arianna touched her hands to her temples. Of course. The man was bound to be a representative of Borghese International, come to audit the remaining assets of the Butterfly.

Quickly, she put Jonathan's picture into the desk drawer. Then she rose to her feet.

What did Dominic Borghese think? That she'd tiptoe out the door with a few bolts of lace under her arm? That she'd tuck a couple of dozen silk teddies under her coat? Perhaps he did business that way, but he had a nerve assuming she would behave like him.

"Tom!" Arianna strode from her office into the adjoining reception area where her assistant was pouring boiling water into a tea pot. "Tom, please print out the year's inventory records and bring them to me."

"The entire inventory? That's an awful lot of data."

"I want all of it, and the sales figures for the same period."

"You've got it."

"And forget the *biscotti*," Arianna said grimly. "Dominic Borghese's sending a flunky to check my integrity. I have to let him in, but I don't have to treat him with courtesy."

"Wrong on all counts, Miss Cabot. No one is questioning your integrity, and I would advise you to treat your guest with the utmost courtesy even if he were, as you say, a flunky."

Arianna's heart leaped. That voice. So deep. So soft. So—so filled with warning.

She took a breath and turned around. Her grandmother stood in the doorway. Beside her was the man Arianna had gone to bed with five years ago.

"Quite right," the *marchesa* said brusquely. "Arianna, where are your manners? No one is questioning anything and you will most assuredly treat our guest with courtesy. *Signore,* this is my granddaughter, Arianna del Vecchio Cabot. Arianna, this is our benefactor, Signore Dominic Borghese."

Arianna gaped. Say something, she told herself desperately. Say anything...

Instead, she dropped to the floor like a stone.

CHAPTER THREE

DOMINIC and the *marchesa* had flown to New York in his private plane.

The *marchesa* had slept most of the way. Dominic had spent the time thinking about the coming encounter with the woman who'd slipped from his bed.

For years, he'd been plagued with questions about her. What was her name? Why had she vanished?

The only thing he'd been sure of was that he'd never taken a woman as he'd taken her. No polite conversation. No pretense at civility. Just heat. Heat and hunger. And pleasure, *Dio,* pleasure beyond anything he'd ever experienced.

And she'd walked out while he slept.

At first, it had puzzled him. After a while, it had angered him. He supposed it was petty. They'd shared a couple of hours in bed. When it was over, after she'd cried out beneath him as he'd emptied himself into her, they'd owed each other nothing.

It was just that waking and finding her gone without leaving a note, a name, a telephone number, having her dismiss him as if he were a beggar in the streets…

Yes, that had made him angry.

Still, the night was history. He'd probably have gone on thinking about it once in a while, but when fate stepped in and the woman in his bed turned out to be the *marchesa's* granddaughter…

Only the gods could have scripted such a tale.

That the *marchesa* wanted him to marry her granddaughter was a bonus. Of course, he had no intention of agreeing to the plan, though he'd yet to tell that to the *marchesa.* He would, when the time was right. Surely, there'd be a way to do it that would help even the score.

Petty? Perhaps, but revenge could be sweet.

As his jet flew through the clouds high over the Atlantic, he'd tried to imagine Arianna's reaction when she saw him. He'd expected her to be shocked, staggered, horrified...

What he hadn't imagined was that she'd take one look at him and pass out.

The *marchesa* screamed. Dominic cursed, rushed forward and caught Arianna before she fell. Her assistant came barreling through the door and added his cries to the old woman's.

Dominic shouldered past them both and laid Arianna on a tapestry-covered sofa. Her face was white and when he clasped her wrist, he felt her pulse racing beneath his fingertips.

The assistant was still making a fuss but the *marchesa* had fallen silent. Her face was pinched and as white as her granddaughter's.

Wonderful, Dominic thought grimly. One woman had fainted and the other was about to do the same, and if the damned fool assistant didn't shut up...

He swung toward him and barked out a single word. *"Silenzio!"*

It worked. The man clapped a hand to his mouth.

"What is your name?"

"T-Tom. Tom B-Bergman."

"Tom. Bring me some cool water."

"There—there's water in that carafe."

"Pour two glasses and give one to the *marchesa.*" Dominic touched the old woman's shoulder. *"Per favore,"* he said gently, "sit down."

To his relief, she didn't argue.

"Is Arianna all right?" she whispered as she sank into a chair beside the sofa.

"Yes, she's fine. She fainted, that's all. Please, take that glass and drink some water."

The *marchesa* nodded again and brought the glass to her lips. Dominic turned to Tom. "Ice," he said crisply. "And a compress."

"A compress? We don't have—"

"Anything, for God's sake. A napkin. A scarf. Something I can fill with ice and hold to Signorina Cabot's forehead, *si?*"

"*Si.* I mean, yes. Yes, sir. Right away."

Arianna moaned softly. Dominic squatted beside the sofa and eased his arm beneath her shoulders. If it weren't for the presence of the old woman, he thought coldly, he'd let her lie there until she recovered consciousness on her own. But the *marchesa* was leaning forward, and the hand that held the glass was shaking.

Dominic smiled reassuringly. "You see? She's coming around already."

Tom bustled into the room with a bowl of ice and a silk teddy. "Will this do? It's the first thing I found."

"It's fine."

Dominic scooped some ice into the teddy and held it to Arianna's forehead. She moaned again and her lashes fluttered. Her eyes opened and met his. The color of her eyes was unusual, like the sky on a soft June morning. An innocent blue, he'd thought that night he'd taken her in his arms.

His mouth twisted. He put down the ice, took the glass of water and held it to her lips as he raised her shoulders from the sofa.

"Drink," he said curtly.

"What—what happened?"

"You passed out. Drink some water."

She took a sip. As she did, she looked at him again and he knew the exact second the pieces fell into place. Her eyes widened. Color rushed to her cheeks.

"You," she whispered.

Dominic smiled tightly. "What a surprise."

Arianna pushed the glass aside and jerked away from his encircling arm.

"Sit up too quickly and you'll faint again."

"Let go of me."

He shrugged indifferently and did as she'd asked. What did he give a damn if she passed out a second time?

"As you wish."

Arianna sat up. Something wet and cold fell into her lap. She picked it up, looked at it and wished she hadn't.

"We had to improvise," Dominic said wryly.

She swung her feet to the floor. The room tilted and she took a deep breath and willed herself not to pass out again. Once was enough. More than enough. To faint at the feet of Dominic Borghese was bad. To do it in front of her grandmother, who looked as if she'd aged a dozen years, was horrendous.

"Nonna." Arianna reached for the *marchesa's* hand. "Are you all right?"

"Never mind me, child. I'm fine. It's you I'm concerned about. What happened? Why did you faint?"

Why, indeed? Arianna hesitated. She could hardly tell her grandmother she'd collapsed because she'd looked up to see the father of her child standing in the doorway.

"Perhaps the signorina saw something that upset her."

Arianna shot a glance at Dominic. He was smiling as if he found the situation amusing. Amusing? To discover that the woman he'd seduced was the same woman he was going to put out of business?

"She didn't have anything to eat today."

Everyone looked at Tom.

"Not a mouthful," he said accusingly. "She's been so busy, preparing for tomorrow's closing... Arianna, won't you let me send out for something?"

"Just bring the coffee and tea for my grandmother and

our—our guest. I'm not hungry. Unless... "Grand-mother?" Arianna said, deliberately ignoring Dominic. "Would you like something to eat?"

"We just had lunch on Signore Borghese's jet." The *marchesa* smiled. "Such a lovely plane, Arianna. Tooled leather seats, low tables..."

"I'm sure it's wonderful," Arianna said politely, "but I'm also sure the *signore* didn't come all this distance so we can talk about his airplane."

"No." The *marchesa* sighed. "He did not. He came to see the Butterfly, now that he owns it."

"He doesn't," Arianna said quickly. "Not quite yet."

"Ah, but I shall by this time tomorrow." Dominic flashed another quick smile. "Does that trouble you, Signorina Cabot? That your beloved Butterfly will belong to me?"

Oh, he was definitely enjoying this. Why? Because she'd left his bed before she could embarrass herself again? It didn't matter. Whatever he thought, whatever she said, she'd lost the Butterfly anyway.

"Yes," she said coolly, "it does."

"Arianna," the *marchesa* said, "for heaven's sake—"

"No, no," Dominic said, "that's all right. I like a woman who speaks her mind." He tucked his hands into his trouser pockets and rocked back a little on his heels. "I'm curious, *signorina*. What bothers you the most about this transaction? That you will lose the Butterfly, or that I will gain it?"

She didn't hesitate. "Both."

"Arianna," the *marchesa* said sharply, "watch your tongue!"

"Signore Borghese might as well hear the truth, grand-mother. It won't change the final outcome." Arianna turned to Dominic. "The Butterfly dates back centuries. From what I know of Borghese International, that won't mean a damn to you."

"You mean, from what you know of me," Dominic said smoothly. "Come now, *signorina,* don't be shy. All of Rome knows that I haven't a history as honorable as yours."

"I'm interested in the Butterfly's honor, not yours. I can't imagine you giving it the individual attention it deserves. All of this—*all* of it," Arianna said, spreading her arms, "will be just another cog in a corporate wheel."

"Meaning I won't run it as you did."

"Exactly."

"Well then, at least it won't go bankrupt and end up in the hands of your creditors."

It was a low blow, but Arianna knew she deserved it. "Believe me, I'd give anything to go back and change what happened."

"Unfortunately, it's impossible to change what we do once we've done it. Surely, even a princess knows that."

Dominic's voice was soft, his words clearly meant to have special meaning for her. A princess. That was what he'd called her that night. She wanted to slap his face, to tell him not to play this game, but her grandmother was watching them with rapt attention.

"That's true, *signore,*" Arianna said politely. "But there are those of us who learn from our mistakes."

"Indeed. But...perhaps you can enlighten me about something, *signorina.*"

Arianna looked at Dominic again. His eyes had narrowed to dark green slits.

"If I can."

"We've met before, haven't we?"

"No." Did she sound calm? How could she, when her heart was racing? "No, we haven't."

"Are you certain? You look so familiar. Perhaps we met in Rome."

"Rome? I don't think so."

"Florence? You do spend time in Florence, don't you?"

"No."

"Arianna, don't be silly." The *marchesa* gave a little laugh. "Of course she spends time in *Firenze,* Signore Borghese. Perhaps..." She looked from Dominic to Arianna. "Is it possible you two met there?"

"We've never met anywhere," Arianna said decisively.

"I never forget a face, *signorina,* especially one so lovely." Dominic frowned. "Wait. It's coming to me. A party. Here, in New York. Five years ago." His smile was smooth as silk. "Do you recall it now? Or shall I tweak your memory a little?"

The room seemed to tilt again. The bastard. Why was he toying with her?

"That won't be necessary, *signore.*"

"We don't need such formality, Arianna. Call me Dominic, please."

"Dominic," she said, though the name seemed to stick in her throat. "I suppose it's possible we met a long time ago."

"We did. I knew it as soon as I saw your photo at your grandmother's *palazzo.*"

"But you never said a word!" The *marchesa* laughed girlishly. "Dominic, how naughty. You should have told me you knew my granddaughter when I asked you—when we discussed business."

"I wanted to surprise you, *marchesa,*" Dominic said, lazily enough that it made Arianna's belly knot.

So, he'd known who she was all along. *That* was why he'd come here, so he could have the pleasure of taking the Butterfly from her in person. Apparently, she'd insulted him by slipping from his bed without a word.

Oh, if she'd only known his identity that night. She'd heard of Dominic Borghese. Who hadn't? And if half the things people whispered about him were true, she'd never have slept with him. The man was a savage...

A savage whose touch she'd never forgotten.

Heat rose in her face.

He was also an arrogant son of a bitch who'd come all this distance to rub her nose in the fact that he was the man taking the Butterfly from her. He wanted to play games? Fine. She'd accommodate him.

Arianna smiled and tucked her hands into the pockets of her silk slacks.

"You know, now that I think about it... Perhaps I do recall meeting you before."

"Really."

"Mmm." She was tempted to bat her lashes, but why push a good thing too far? Instead, she gave him a big, bright smile.

"Unfortunately, I can't be certain. I meet so many people. You understand. Sometimes it's difficult to remember them all."

"Unfortunate, indeed."

"On the other hand, if our meeting was memorable, I wouldn't need reminding, would I?"

A muscle ticked in his jaw. "In that case," he said softly, "perhaps I can find ways to refresh your memory."

The warning was clear. *Don't underestimate me,* he was saying, *or you'll regret it.*

He was right. What was the matter with her? You didn't play dangerous games with a man like this, especially if you had a secret to protect. Twenty-four hours, that was all, and the Butterfly would belong to him. She could handle things for one day.

"For heaven's sake!" The *marchesa* looked from Arianna to Dominic. "What is all this? Do you two know each other or not?"

Arianna held her breath and waited. The next move had to be Dominic's. Seconds crept past and then he smiled at her grandmother, took her hand and brought it to his lips.

"We did meet once, a long time ago. I'm afraid your granddaughter has forgotten me, but I haven't forgotten her.

What man could forget a woman who is the image of you, *marchesa?*''

The *marchesa* blushed. Arianna had never seen her grandmother blush in her entire life. Without question, the man had a way with women.

''What charm you have, Dominic. No wonder one hears such naughty whispers about you.''

''What you hear is usually the product of someone's imagination.'' He grinned. ''It's what you *don't* hear that's really interesting.''

The *marchesa* giggled. Arianna tried not to roll her eyes but he must have known what she was thinking because he flashed her the kind of smile that made her want to slap it off his face.

''Coffee,'' Tom sang out as he breezed in with a silver tray in his hands. ''And tea.'' He glanced at Arianna. ''And some wonderful *biscotti.*''

Saved by the bell, Arianna thought, and busied herself by playing hostess.

Dominic left the women in late afternoon.

He said his goodbyes politely, bending over the *marchesa's* hand, then Arianna's, though that involved a determined, if invisible, tug of war as she tried to jerk her fingers from his. Eventually, he applied just enough pressure so she finally gave up fighting.

Once on the street, he felt like a man let out of a cage.

No wonder the *marchesa* was trying to marry off her granddaughter. The old woman wanted more than his money. She wanted a man to tame a wildcat.

Dio, he'd be sorry for the fool who married her.

Some poor idiot would surely be taken in by that stunning face, that lush body, those innocent-seeming eyes. And what a shock that man would have when he realized he'd married a woman with a sharp tongue, a prickly disposition…and a taste for falling into bed with men she didn't know and had no interest in seeing again.

Dominic waved away his chauffeur. His head was full of questions. He needed to walk. To think. It had been, to put it mildly, one hell of an afternoon.

Traffic heading uptown was heavy. Cars and trucks slipped past each other with inches to spare; pedestrians hurried along the narrow streets without concern for red lights or green. Dominic followed suit. He felt at home in New York. In many ways, the city reminded him of Rome. The impatient traffic. The energy and vitality of the streets.

Energy and vitality. Those words could also describe Arianna and what had drawn him to her five years ago. She'd been out of place at that party, stalking the room with impatience, her smile wooden, her eyes showing her boredom.

She hadn't been bored in his arms that night.

She hadn't been bored today, either. First she'd gone toe to toe with him in a verbal duel. Once she'd realized he wasn't to be trifled with, she'd done her best to act civilly, but he'd seen straight through the polite words and courteous smiles.

Arianna Cabot loathed him.

Dominic stepped off the curb. A horn honked angrily. He took a quick step back as a taxi whizzed past.

Amazing, that she'd gone to bed with him without checking his pedigree. Or maybe she had. Maybe she'd known who he was and wanted to see what it was like to sleep with a barbarian.

Either way, she'd made her point. He was good enough to sleep with but not good enough for anything else. She'd all but curled her lip each time she'd looked at him this afternoon. Not that she'd looked at him very often. Once her assistant brought in that tray she'd done her best to ignore him, even when the *marchesa* tried to include him in the conversation.

Arianna hadn't been able to hide her disdain.

In turn, he'd behaved as if he hadn't noticed...but he had. *Dio,* she infuriated him! Did she really think she could get away with treating him like that? She couldn't. He wouldn't permit it. He'd made that promise to himself the first time—the only time—a woman had made a fool of him.

How old had he been then? Seventeen? Eighteen? It had been summer then, too. He'd been working for a contractor, laying bricks at a rich man's villa just outside Rome. The owner of the villa had a daughter. She'd watched him working shirtless under the blazing sun for almost a week. Then she'd set out to seduce him.

It had taken no effort at all.

He was young and hot-blooded. She was sophisticated and beautiful. She'd welcomed him to her bed every night for two weeks until, with the foolishness of youth, he'd told her he'd fallen in love with her and asked if she loved him, too.

"Me?" she'd said incredulously. "In love with *you?"* And she'd laughed and laughed...

Dominic walked faster.

No way would he let history repeat itself. He'd tolerated Arianna's behavior for the *marchesa's* sake, but politeness only demanded so much of a man. That he should have endured her coldness, the icy glances meant to remind him that she was an aristocrat and he was a nobody...

A nobody who held the future of the del Vecchio family in his hands.

She had the bloodlines, but he had the money.

Dominic paused at the curb. His limousine glided to a stop alongside. His driver didn't get out. The man had been with him long enough to know that his boss didn't like shows of subservience in anyone.

Although right now, Dominic thought grimly, as he climbed into the car and it headed toward Fifth Avenue, right now, watching Arianna Cabot do a little bowing and scraping would be a pleasure.

The amazing thing was that he'd managed to control his temper today.

How many times had he almost shot from his chair, grabbed the ice princess by the shoulders and reminded her that she hadn't found him so distasteful the night she'd slept with him?

How many times had he come close to proving it by clasping that beautiful face in his hands and kissing her until her mouth lost its haughty stiffness and melted under his?

He'd kept his temper because it just wasn't worth losing it. He didn't want anything from Arianna. Not her uselessly old-fashioned business, not her body, not even a show of respect.

All he wanted was payback. Wasn't that what the Americans called it? And he'd have it tomorrow.

The car glided to a stop outside the hotel where Dominic kept a suite—the suite he'd taken Arianna to that night.

"Will you be wanting the car this evening, Mr. Borghese?"

Dominic shook his head. "No, George. Put it in the garage and take the night off."

"See you tomorrow morning, then. Seven o'clock, right?"

"Right."

Tomorrow morning, Dominic thought as he rode the private elevator to the penthouse, he would go back to the Butterfly and at the moment the place was supposed to become his, he'd tell the *marchesa* that he didn't want it and he didn't want her granddaughter, either.

He'd be damned if he'd take an old woman's sole asset. As for marrying Arianna…did the *marchesa* really believe he'd give up his freedom, give up choosing his own wife, for the supposed benefit of joining his blood with the del Vecchios?

Dominic yanked off his suit jacket and tie and tossed them on a chair in the foyer. He walked into the living room as he unbuttoned his shirt collar and rolled back his cuffs.

The truth was, the *marchesa* wouldn't have looked at him twice if she still had money.

Dominic dumped ice into a glass, opened a bottle and poured himself a finger of Kentucky bourbon. It was a taste he'd acquired when he'd spent a couple of years in the States, though he hardly ever indulged it. It was important to have a clear head at all times.

Besides, he'd seen too much of what alcohol could do to people while he was growing up.

Still, a small celebration seemed called for, considering that tomorrow was going to be filled with surprises for Arianna.

Dominic stepped out onto the terrace and gazed down at Central Park sprawled far below him, a calm oasis of green in the concrete hurly-burly of the city. He lifted the whiskey to his lips and let the first sip warm his belly.

The bittersweet truth about the *marchesa's* "merger" suggestion was that *if* the del Vecchio fortune were intact, *if* he'd met Arianna the usual way, *if* they'd fallen in love— whatever that meant—*if* he'd asked her to marry him, the old woman would have moved heaven and earth to keep the marriage from taking place.

His blood would never be blue, but his bank account was fat. That was all that mattered to people like the del Vecchois.

Dominic lifted the glass to his lips and frowned when he realized it was empty. He went inside the living room, poured himself a second drink, then took the bottle outside to watch the sky darken and the lights in the park flicker on while he poured a third.

By the time he fell into bed, he didn't give a damn about anything but that moment tomorrow when he'd look Arianna in the eye and tell her his lawyers had already drawn up the necessary papers that would, in effect, cancel out the loan.

He didn't want the Butterfly. He certainly didn't want Arianna.

He'd tell her that. It was why he'd come all this distance, so that he could enjoy the look on her face when she learned that her grandmother had tried to sell her to him— and her reaction when he told her he'd sooner marry an alley cat than take her as a wife.

Dominic yawned, rolled over and fell soundly asleep.

CHAPTER FOUR

DOMINIC awoke to the insistent ringing of a bell.

He fumbled for the alarm clock and hit the off switch, but that didn't stop the noise. Neither did slamming the clock with his fist. Finally, he struggled up against the pillows, winced at the throbbing pain in his temples, and grabbed the telephone.

"What?" he barked.

"Buon giorno."

It was the *marchesa*. Dominic looked blearily at the clock. It was 4:55 in the morning.

"Marchesa." He cleared his throat. "I hate to sound unsociable, but—"

"Did I wake you, *signore?"*

Dominic closed his eyes. "As a matter of fact—"

"My apologies. I know it's early. I waited all night, as long as I could… Oh, Dominic. I made a mistake. I should not have done it, I know, but—"

"Marchesa." Gingerly, Dominic touched his hand to his head. Surely a man did not deserve such pain even if he'd been foolish enough to drink too much bourbon whiskey. *"Marchesa,* please, speak more slowly."

"Per favore, Dominic, address me by my name. I am Emilia."

Hell. All of a sudden, she wanted him to call her by her given name? The throbbing in his head got worse. What did the old woman want?

"Emilia," he said carefully, "perhaps you've forgotten the time difference here in New—"

"Listen to me, Dominic. I have created a problem."

The *marchesa*—Emilia—began talking, but she didn't

46

slow down. If anything, her words took on added speed and urgency.

Half-listening, Dominic clutched the phone to his ear and made his way to the bathroom. He rummaged through the medicine cabinet for a bottle of aspirin, tapped three tablets—four, he thought, wincing—into the palm of his hand and gulped them down.

Why had he drunk so much last night? He wasn't a drinker and there was nothing to celebrate. He'd go to today's meeting, make his announcement about the immediate liquidation of the company, then fly home. Never mind mentioning her grandmother's absurd marriage plan to Arianna. He had no time for something as self-indulgent as revenge. When he could get a word in, he'd simply tell the *marchesa* he wasn't interested. Then he could go back to Rome and put this ridiculous episode behind him.

The *marchesa* was still talking. About what? Dominic thought wearily, and headed for the kitchen.

"Emilia," he said, interrupting the stream of words, "as a special favor to me, take a couple of breaths and start again, yes? Tell me what's wrong."

What was wrong, the old woman said, was that she, and she alone, had ruined everything.

"Everything!" Her voice shook. "And I am so terribly sorry."

Dominic turned on the kitchen lights. One-handed, he took down the coffee, spooned some into the filter, changed his mind and spooned in more, then filled the pot with water.

"You cannot imagine how I regret my error!"

Actually, he could. He regretted his errors, too. He should never have come to New York, never have let the *marchesa* spend a moment thinking he'd really collect on the loan or so much as consider her ludicrous suggestion that he marry Arianna.

"Dominic? Do you hear me?"

"I hear you, Emilia. What error?"

"I—how do you say it? I let the cat out of the bag. Last night, at dinner, I told Arianna of our plans."

Dominic sighed and sat down at the kitchen counter. Was he going to have to drag each word from her? "What plans?"

"Our merger plans," the *marchesa* said, with more than a touch of impatience. "I told Arianna you were going to propose to her."

"You told her..." Dominic shot to his feet, took the phone from his ear and scowled at it as if the instrument was actually the *marchesa*. "But we had no plans."

"Of course we did. You and Arianna..."

"There is no me and Arianna. I never said I would agree to your proposition!"

"You never said you would not."

"You overstepped yourself, madam," Dominic said sharply. "I have no intention of asking your granddaughter to marry me."

"Well, you should have spoken sooner," the *marchesa* said in icy tones. "Not that it matters now. Arianna laughed when I told her she was to become your wife."

A muscle knotted in Dominic's cheek. "Did she, indeed?"

"Yes. It was as if I had told her the world's best joke."

"I see." The pot was filling with coffee. Dominic shoved a mug under the black, almost viscous stream. "Your granddaughter finds the idea of marriage to me amusing?"

"More than that. She said... Never mind. It does not matter."

"No. It doesn't." Dominic paused. "But I'd like to hear it anyway."

"I don't think so."

His hand tightened on the cup. "Tell me what she said, Emilia."

''She said—she said that she would sooner marry a Martian.''

''A charming image,'' Dominic said coldly.

''I am sorry, but you insisted on knowing.''

''I did, yes.'' Hot coffee sloshed over the rim of the cup onto Dominic's fingers, but he didn't feel it. ''And an interesting choice, since I doubt that your beloved granddaughter would be happy as the wife of a creature with alien anatomy.''

''I do not understand.''

''You don't have to.''

''No,'' the old woman said, as if his rudeness was to be expected. ''I suppose not. I should have left this to you, Dominic. Perhaps you would have been able to convince her.''

''I just told you I was not going to propose marriage to Arianna. Do you understand?''

''What I understand is that I am going to lose *La Farfalla*.''

''We will discuss that,'' Dominic said coldly, ''when we all meet this morning.''

''You and I shall meet. Arianna will not be there.''

''What do you mean, she won't be there? Your granddaughter is a part of this, *Marchesa*. I expect her to attend the meeting.''

''I would have assumed she would *want* to attend, but she refuses.''

Dominic gripped the phone more tightly. ''And I insist. I'm not offering her a choice. Tell her that.''

''I cannot.''

''Then *I'll* tell her.''

''You can't, *signore*. My granddaughter and I had words. I said some harsh things. I accused her of having forgotten the importance of honor.''

''And you were right.''

"The point is, after our quarrel Arianna decided to leave."

"Leave? *Leave?*"

"She went to her house in the country late last night."

Dominic scraped his hand through his hair. This was impossible. How could a straightforward plan become so complicated?

"Give me her telephone number. I'll call and make it clear that she must return to the city."

"I don't know it. I didn't even know she had a country house." The *marchesa's* words were touched with acid. "It would seem there's a great deal I did not know about my granddaughter. For instance, until yesterday I thought you and she were strangers."

"Believe me," Dominic said brusquely, "we are."

"That is not what Arianna says. She admitted that she remembers meeting you, but she won't discuss it because she says it was a brief, unpleasant encounter."

"Indeed." Dominic's tone was silken. "What else did she say?"

"Only that she has no wish to see you again." The *marchesa's* sigh whispered through the telephone. "Truly, I regret saying these things, but how else can I convince you that she would not change her mind about attending the meeting even if you could reach her...which you cannot."

"Your granddaughter has lived in America too long, Emilia. You're right. She needs a lesson in deportment and a reminder of her obligations." Dominic reached for a pad and pencil. "Where is this country house?"

"I don't know its precise location. Outside the city. That is all I can tell you."

Outside the city. That certainly narrowed things down. Arianna Cabot's house could be anywhere within three states and God only knew how many hundreds of miles.

"Is this a problem? Is there a reason my granddaughter must be present today?"

Dominic almost laughed. Could a man's battered pride be called a problem?

"Actually," he said calmly, glancing at the clock, "now that I think about it, neither of you has to be present."

"What a relief! My quarrel with Arianna exhausted me. I will be very happy to leave this place."

"I can arrange that right now, if you wish." Dominic spoke quickly, as if taking the time to consider what he was about to do might be a mistake. "My driver can pick you up and take you to the airport. My pilot will fly you home."

"I do not wish to inconvenience you, Dominic."

"It's not an inconvenience. I'm going to stay on for a few days. I have some business here, but that needn't affect you."

"Well, if you're certain…"

"I am."

"Thank you, Dominic. And again, my apologies for spoiling your plans."

"No, no. *My* apologies for my bad temper. You had no way of knowing I didn't intend to ask your granddaughter to marry me."

"To be honest, I'm not surprised. I thought it was too much to hope for."

Dominic nodded. He was calmer, as was the *marchesa*. Now was the time to tell her he wasn't going to call in the loan, either.…

But he didn't.

"My driver will contact you, Emilia. You can tell him when to come for you."

"*Mille grazie.*"

"You're welcome."

Dominic hung up the phone. He drank more coffee, black as sludge and with the same consistency. Why hadn't he told the *marchesa* that she didn't have to worry about the loan? The Butterfly was all the old woman had. He wasn't going to take it from her, he simply wanted to give Arianna a scare. Just a settling of scores to make up for the endless nights he'd spent thinking about her.

His hand tightened around the coffee cup.

She'd laughed at the idea of marrying him. But she hadn't laughed when he made love to her. She'd made the soft, breathless sounds of a woman being pleasured by a man, sounds that still drove him half out of his mind when he remembered them.

The message was clear. He was beneath the princess's notice, except in bed. She'd sooner marry a creature with three eyes and eight tentacles, marry *anybody,* than him.

Dominic dumped his coffee in the sink.

Arianna needed another lesson in humility. And he had time for that before heading home.

Back in his bedroom, Dominic stripped off his shorts and stepped into an icy shower. It didn't cool his anger but he hadn't expected it to. What he wanted was to get himself under control so that he could hone his rage and use it efficiently.

There was always a way to defeat an enemy. You just had to calm down enough to determine what it was.

Dominic got out of the shower and wrapped a towel around his hips. What was the name of Arianna's assistant? Tim. No. Tom. Tom what? Berg. Berger. Bergman, he thought, snapping his fingers. That was it. Bergman.

The number was easy to find in the directory. The phone rang half a dozen times before Bergman answered.

No sir, he didn't know a thing about his employer's country place. Yes sir, he had an emergency phone number for her, but he couldn't—

A few well-chosen words and it turned out that he could. Dominic could almost see the man jump to attention, and this was one of those times jumping to attention was exactly what he wanted.

Bergman gave him a number, Dominic scribbled it down

and made a call to a private detective in Manhattan that Borghese International sometimes employed.

It took slightly more than an hour to get the necessary information, more than enough time to put on jeans, a blue short-sleeved soccer shirt and moccasins, and to arrange for the delivery of a car.

Finally, he called his pilot and told him to ready the plane, and his driver to tell him he'd be taking the *marchesa* to the airport.

"By the way, George..." Dominic frowned at the address he'd written down during his conversation with the detective. "Do you happen to know the quickest route to Stanton, Connecticut? Yes? Great. Uh-huh. I don't suppose you'd know where Wildflower Road is... No, that's fine. I'll find it."

Dominic hung up the phone and headed for the door.

Moments later, he was in a rented black SUV, racing toward a small town in the rolling Connecticut hills.

Arianna loved her house.

It dated back to the 1930s, which made it completely unfashionable. The celebrities who bought property in this part of New England preferred authentic colonials, even if they were falling down.

Her house was sturdily built. It had wooden floors and a brick fireplace, and was tucked against a stand of pine trees at the end of a long, unpaved road. Hardly anybody ever drove up that road except for Jonathan's nanny and an occasional delivery van.

This was a world far removed from the hustle and bustle of Manhattan, and Arianna loved it. She hadn't expected to: she'd only bought the place so she could raise her son in privacy, but after a couple of months the house felt more like home than anyplace she'd lived since she was a little girl.

The quiet of the woods always soothed her soul.

But not today, Arianna thought as she tore leaves of Bibb lettuce into a wooden bowl. Jonathan wasn't here. He'd gone fishing with a friend and the friend's father. A good thing, too, because her little boy could read her like a book. She didn't want him to see the anger she'd suppressed…anger at the man he would never know was his father.

Arianna tore a leaf in smaller pieces with more force than necessary.

She was almost as furious now as she'd been driving here. Except for the hour she'd sat beside her sleeping son last night and the time they'd spent together at breakfast this morning, the blood still pumped hot and fast through her veins.

Had Dominic really thought she'd marry him? Had her grandmother thought it, too?

Incredibly, the answer seemed to be yes. Bad enough Dominic imagined she'd trade herself for the Butterfly, but that the *marchesa* should have thought she'd do it…

"I'm an innocent bystander, Arianna," her grandmother had insisted. "I am simply transmitting a proposition. Surely, you do not think this was my idea."

Arianna plunged a paring knife into a tomato.

Maybe not. But the *marchesa* didn't seem all that offended by the message she'd brought from Dominic.

"What message?" Arianna had asked. "Has he decided that taking the Butterfly from us isn't enough? Does he want a pound of flesh, too?"

Her grandmother had ignored the outburst. "Signore Borghese says to tell you he will forgive the loan under certain conditions."

The shock of those words, the hope they'd offered, had made her heart skip a beat. Maybe Dominic Borghese wasn't quite the rat she'd thought.

"What conditions?"

"He wants you to agree to become his wife," her grandmother had said bluntly.

Arianna's mouth had dropped open. "He wants what?"

"Dominic wishes to marry you."

"What kind of joke is this, *Nonna?*"

"I thought it was a joke, too. But the *signore* is quite serious."

"I should marry him? That—that walking collection of conceits? A man I don't know, don't like, don't want to see again in this lifetime?"

She'd said a few more things, most even less polite, and only stopped when she realized it wasn't fair to blame the message on the messenger. But when her grandmother used the pause to drop in some words explaining why it might be a smart idea rather than a foolish one, Arianna had exploded.

"Foolish doesn't even come close! It's idiotic, insane and impossible."

"Signore Borghese could give you a comfortable life," her grandmother had said quietly.

"I am quite comfortable in my life already, thank you very much. How could you even think—"

"And you are the last of our line. We need an heir."

That hurt. There was a del Vecchio heir, but the *marchesa* didn't know it. Not yet.

"I'm sure there will be," Arianna said stiffly. "Someday."

"Someday," the *marchesa* scoffed. "When? A woman your age should have a husband."

"A woman *my…?* For God's sake, *Nonna,* I'm only twenty-nine!"

"Having a man in your life and in your bed would be good for you."

A picture flashed in Arianna's mind of Dominic, taking her in his arms. Moving over her, kneeling between her thighs, his body naked and strong and breathtakingly beautiful...

"I don't need a man in either place," she'd said coldly. "I'm doing fine as I am."

"Think of the Butterfly. You would keep it."

"Do you really imagine I want the Butterfly so badly I'd sell my soul to the devil or my body to his emissary? I'm sorry you're losing the Butterfly, *Nonna,* of course, but—"

"In times past," the *marchesa* had said with a regal lift of her chin, "a merger between powerful families was desirable. Our name is old and our lineage proud. Dominic may not carry the blood of the ancient Borgheses but he is dynamic and powerful. Can't you see the benefits of merging the two?"

"Are you saying you'd be happy if I accepted this ridiculous proposition?"

"Certainly not. I am simply reminding you that there are things one does for reasons that go beyond one's own desires."

"I won't trade our name for his bank account."

"The combining of the Borghese and del Vecchio houses would not be as crass as you make it sound."

"You *do* want me to do this! Well, I won't. I'd sooner rot. I'd sooner—I'd sooner marry a creature from Mars!"

"As you wish, child. I'll give Dominic your answer, but more diplomatically."

"You tell it to him exactly as I phrased it," Arianna had said furiously. She'd gone on for a few more seconds before she'd suddenly remembered her grandmother's fragile health and advanced age. *"Nonna,"* she'd said, "I love you with all my heart and I don't want to argue with you or upset you. Perhaps it would be best if I didn't come to tomorrow's meeting. Actually, there's no reason for me to be there."

Her grandmother had sighed. "You're right. Perhaps you should stay away."

Arianna sliced a scored cucumber into the bowl.

That was when she'd slipped up and said she'd go to her country house for the weekend. For the first time, the *marchesa* had seemed surprised.

"You never mentioned a country house before."

"Didn't I?" Arianna had said, as casually as she could. "I guess the subject never came up."

They'd chatted about inconsequential things long enough to heal the breach in their relationship. Then Arianna had left her grandmother's hotel, phoned Susan and begun the long drive to the country, which she'd hoped would calm her.

It hadn't.

One way or another, she had to get the anger out of her system by midafternoon. Jeff Gooding had promised he'd have the boys back by then.

"With lots of big fish for supper," Jonathan had said.

"*Real* big fish," Jeff's son had echoed.

Jeff had winked over the boys' heads. "You might want to figure on something for standby, just in case the fish don't cooperate."

Arianna smiled. What he'd meant was that the kids never caught anything at the pond. Jeff did, sometimes, but he'd told her the boys always made him release his catch. Fishing was an excuse to dangle lines in the water and talk man-talk. It had nothing to do with anything as awful as actually hauling fish out of the water and killing them.

Jeff Gooding was a widower, a nice guy who was generous with his time and often included Jonathan in his plans.

He's got a thing for you, Susan always teased.

But Arianna didn't have a "thing" for him. He wasn't complex, like Dominic, or strong, like Dominic, or exciting, like...

Dammit! Arianna scowled as she quartered a tomato. She had Dominic on the brain. Jeff wasn't cold, selfish and egotistical like Dominic, either. He was a pillar of the community and a good role model for Jonathan. If there was one thing her little boy lacked, it was a male role model.

If she married Dominic Borghese, her son would have a role model. He'd have the man who was his very own father.

"Arianna."

Arianna's head snapped toward the screen door. Dominic stood on the porch, his tall figure limned by the sun.

The forgotten paring knife sliced into her finger. Bright red blood splattered over the white marble cutting board. She stared blankly at the blood, at the knife...

"Il mio Dio!"

Dimly, like the background noise of a radio turned low, Arianna heard the splinter of wood as Dominic put his shoulder against the frame. The door flew open.

"Do you make a habit of fainting?" he said gruffly, as his arms closed around her.

No, she wanted to tell him, only when I'm with you. But she wasn't foolish enough to say that as he carried her from the kitchen to the parlor, where he eased her onto the old-fashioned love seat near the fireplace.

"I'm fine," she said in a thready voice. "Just let me sit here for a minute."

"Apply pressure against the cut and put your head down." She felt his hand guide her fingers to the wound. "Like that. And don't move," he added as he left her.

He sounded like a man accustomed to giving commands and having them obeyed. Arianna was a woman who never took commands, but she did now. Following a sensible order was better than falling on her face, especially since she'd already done that once in his presence.

She heard his footsteps returning. He tied a strip of cloth around her finger.

"Thank you. That's—"

"Sit still."

"I'm trying to tell you, I'm okay."

"Of course. That's the reason your face is as white as paper." He took her hand, examined it and muttered something in an Italian dialect she didn't understand. "The cut looks deep. It might need stitches, and you might need a tetanus shot."

"I don't need a shot, and the cut isn't deep."

"How do you know how deep it is until you see it? Why must you argue with everything I say?"

"I'm not arguing. I'm simply telling you…" She took a breath. She *was* arguing, and there was no reason for it. She didn't have to explain herself to him. "Let go of my hand so I can see the cut."

"Will you pass out if you do?"

"No. I don't know why…" She did know. She'd been thinking about her son, about Dominic, and then she'd looked up and he was there, so big, so masculine, so real. "You surprised me, that's all."

His mouth twisted, just the way Jonathan's had when she'd told him she didn't think that Godzilla could really, truly destroy Tokyo.

"If you faint again, I'm taking you to the nearest hospital."

"I didn't faint. I *won't* faint." Arianna jerked her hand free of Dominic's. The cut was small, as she'd thought, and not very deep. The blood had already changed from a flow to a slow ooze. "It's fine," she said briskly. "Now, please leave my house."

"You need a proper bandage."

"I don't."

"Where are they?"

"I said—"

"I heard you. Where are the bandages?"

Unbelievable! He really thought he could boss her around in her own home. She opened her mouth to tell him that, then thought better of it. What mattered was getting him out the door, and fast.

"In the medicine cabinet in the bathroom," she snapped. "Down the hall, first door on the left."

She sat tapping her foot until he returned with a small packet, tore it open and put the bandage over the cut.

"That's better."

Insolent bastard, she thought, but just then his fingers brushed hers and a rush of electricity sizzled through her. She snatched back her hand, as annoyed at herself as she already was at him.

"I'm glad you think so. Now go away."

"Such a generous display of gratitude," he said, his sarcastic tone a match for hers. "I'll go when we've finished our business."

"Didn't the *marchesa* tell you? I'm not going to participate in whatever little victory ceremony you planned for today."

"Victory ceremony?"

Dominic got to his feet and folded his arms. Arianna tried not to notice how he towered over her. He was wearing jeans and a short-sleeved shirt that revealed muscled, tanned forearms lightly dusted with black hair.

Manhattan overflowed with men who wore outfits like this on weekends. She supposed it was to make them look young and fit, but she'd always thought such styles just made men accustomed to custom-tailored suits look slightly foolish.

Dominic didn't look foolish. Not that it mattered. How he looked was what had gotten her in trouble in the first place.

"Yes," she said, "victory ceremony. That's the reason you came to New York, isn't it? To enjoy seeing my face as you took the Butterfly from me?"

It was too close to the truth to deny. Dominic narrowed his gaze on those innocent-looking blue eyes.

"Your grandmother offered it as collateral."

"Yes, well, that was her mistake."

"It would seem she made another mistake." His eyes

glittered. "She tells me you found her merger suggestion amusing."

"Her merger sugg…" Arianna flushed. "The marriage thing, you mean. Come now, *signore*. Surely you don't expect me to think…" Her color deepened at the amused smile that curved his mouth. "She would never have come up with such an idea."

"And you think I would?" He laughed. "Trust me, Arianna. You're beautiful and I enjoyed the night we spent together, but I'd hardly give up my freedom to have you."

"Have me?" God, how despicable this man was! "Believe me, I'm not for sale." She shot to her feet, marched into the kitchen and picked up the salad bowl. "And I wouldn't marry you if my life depended on it."

"How about if your grandmother's future depended on it?"

She swung toward him, the bowl clutched in her hands. "What do you mean?"

"I lent your grandmother money. She was supposed to repay it in kind, not with the dubious honor of your hand in marriage."

"I don't believe that's what she tried to do. Besides, she *is* repaying the loan."

"She owes me three million dollars."

"You're getting the Butterfly."

"It's not worth three million dollars."

Arianna lifted her chin. "Don't blame me if you made a bad bargain, *signore*."

"It seemed like the right thing to do at the time."

"Did it?" Arianna put down the bowl and slapped her hands on her hips. "Why did you lend her so much money in the first place? Did you find out who I was after that night? Was this all some sick scheme to get even with me for walking out on you?"

Dominic's eyes narrowed. "How about you? Did you know who I was when you came on to me at that party?

Were you an appetizer, meant to sweeten the deal before the *marchesa* approached me with her request for money?''

"You bastard!" Arianna's eyes filled with angry tears. That she'd gone to bed with a man like this made her feel sick. "Do you really think I'd sell myself so cheaply?"

"No, probably not, or why would you have slunk away without telling me your name? Maybe you simply went slumming that night, and now you see that the price is higher than you expected."

The price she'd paid was an unplanned pregnancy, but he'd never know that. How right she'd been not to have tried to identify the man who'd fathered her son. Jonathan was hers. She loved him with all her heart—loved him as fiercely, as intensely, as she despised Dominic Borghese.

And she had to get Dominic out of here, before their child returned.

"All right." She took a step back, as if putting some distance between them would help. "You came to New York to get even. Well, you've succeeded. I was wrong that night. That's what you wanted to hear, isn't it?"

Was it? How could he have known it wouldn't be that simple? That everything would change in this moment?

Five years ago, they'd been equals. A man and woman caught up in passion, wanting each other and not giving a damn about the rest of the world. Now, she was a del Vecchio princess who'd been offered for sale to a peasant.

The rules had changed.

The look on her face when she saw him at the door, that mix of fear and loathing, twisted inside him like a knife. Her desperation to get rid of him now, as if his very presence might contaminate her home, fueled his anger.

A man could let anger consume him, or he could use it. Dominic had learned that early.

"Say something," Arianna demanded. "Don't just stand there with that—that look on your face. I've apologized. What more do you want?"

Dominic didn't hesitate. "I want you to become my wife."

CHAPTER FIVE

IT WAS too much.

Arianna had endured almost twenty-four hours of lunacy and this was…

A bad joke? A madman's taunt? She looked at Dominic. He seemed cool, self-possessed, and entirely sane.

Maybe she was the one having the problem.

"You want me to…" She couldn't even say the words. "You want me to do what?"

"I want you to become my wife."

Become his wife? Well, of course. She should have known that he'd propose after everything he'd just said, that the idea was not his but her grandmother's, that he'd never give up his freedom to have her—as if she were an object that *could* be had—after all that, of course he'd propose.

They didn't know each other, didn't like each other, had nothing in common except a son he'd never know existed… Why wouldn't he want her to be his wife?

Arianna began to laugh. What else could you do when the whole world had gone mad?

Dominic's eyes narrowed to slits. "You find my proposition amusing, *signorina?*"

At least he hadn't dignified it by calling it a proposal, she thought, and laughed harder.

"*Basta,*" he growled. "There's nothing funny about this."

He was right. Actually, this was horrible. She took a couple of deep breaths.

"No, there isn't." The hysterical laughter drained away. Arianna folded her arms and looked up into that coldly set

63

face. "Maybe you'd like to tell me what form of humiliation you expect me to endure next."

"Asking a woman for her hand is hardly asking her to endure humiliation."

Neither was being trapped in your own kitchen with the father of your child, when that child could be home at any minute. The timing of a trip to the pond was hard to predict. Jeff and the kids could be gone for hours, but if the boys got bored or the weather turned chilly…

Never mind trying to figure out what Dominic was up to. All that mattered was getting him out the door. He couldn't see Jonathan. For one thing, he'd tell the *marchesa*. For another…

For another, her son looked like his father.

Arianna had never realized it. Maybe she hadn't wanted to, but she could see the resemblance now. They had the same dark, slightly curling hair; the same full mouth; the same classic Roman nose.

But those things didn't make a man and a boy father and son.

She knew women who reached a certain age, gave up hoping to meet Mr. Right and turned to sperm banks to create the children they wanted.

As soon as she'd realized how much she wanted her baby, Arianna had thought of the child in her womb as having been conceived with the help of an anonymous donor. Now that she knew the identity of the man who'd impregnated her, knew that he was an unfeeling, inflexible egotist who took pleasure in wielding his power, she was more convinced than ever that the only parent her boy would ever know—or need—was her.

Dominic was playing head games because she'd nicked his ego.

Maybe he hoped she'd panic. Pass out at his feet again. Well, he'd wait forever. He was up to something and whatever it was, she could handle it.

"Still no answer?" He took a step toward her. "Perhaps you're waiting for me to say it again. I want you to marry me."

Arianna smiled, picked up a bunch of carrots and turned on the water in the sink.

"Nice try," she said politely, "but wasted."

"I beg your pardon?"

"Do you get your kicks trying to shock people? This 'I want you to be my wife' thing. That stroll into my office yesterday. 'Hi, I'm the man who seduced you and oh, by the way, I'm here to take your grandmother's company from her.'"

"Be careful what you say, Arianna."

"What didn't you like? Being reminded of how you got me into bed—or how you set up my grandmother?"

"I set up no one. I'm not a bank. I don't solicit borrowers. Your grandmother came to me for money, I took pity on her and we made a deal. As for seduction... If you need reminding of what happened that night, I'll oblige you."

He moved just enough so that she felt her heart hammer against her ribs. She swung toward him, brandishing the carrots like a weapon.

"Stay where you are!"

Dominic looked at the carrots and raised his eyebrows. Arianna flushed, tossed the carrots in the sink and shut off the water. The idea was to show him he couldn't rattle her. That meant holding her ground, no matter what.

"Let's not argue over semantics. What happened between us is old news. As for my grandmother... She handles her own affairs. If she was foolish enough to borrow three million dollars from you, that's that."

"Unfortunately for the del Vecchios, it isn't."

"What's that supposed to mean?"

"You heard my proposition. I'm still waiting for an answer."

"You mean, will I marry you?" She flashed a smile.

"No, I will not. Is that clear enough or would you like me to say it in Italian?

"I know something that might change your mind."

"Nothing could possibly—"

"The *marchesa* is penniless."

She stared at him. "Don't be ridiculous. She can't be."

"She's as close to flat broke as one can be and still put food on the table."

"That's impossible."

"Because she's a del Vecchio?" He smiled in a way that made her breath catch.

"Because she has a fortune. A *palazzo*. Land. Paintings by old masters. Jewels. She has—"

"She has nothing. The *palazzo* is mortgaged to the hilt. The paintings and jewels have gone to the highest bidder. Think, Arianna. There have been signs. Did you choose not to see them?"

"What signs? Have you taken to reading tea leaves? If my grandmother had sold anything…" She stopped, stared at him in dawning horror. She thought of the Tintoretto that no longer hung in the great hall of the *palazzo,* the Rembrandt that was gone from the salon. The *marchesa* said she'd lent them to a museum. She thought of a ruby pendant, a diamond necklace, other jewels her grandmother no longer wore. Too expensive to insure, she'd said, when Arianna asked about them.

She stared into Dominic's eyes. By now, she knew that Dominic Borghese was a lot of things she didn't like, but instinct told her he wasn't a liar.

"Ohmygod," she whispered.

"Indeed," he said dryly. "But God didn't put her in this position."

"No. *You* did!"

"I had nothing to do with your grandmother's financial situation."

He was right. If anyone had done this to the *marchesa,*

it was she. Did she say it aloud? Did Dominic read what he saw flash across her face? Either way, he spoke before she could.

"It wasn't anything you did."

"I talked her into all kinds of expenses." She swung away from him and clutched the edge of the counter. "New designers. More expensive fabrics."

"Listen to me." Dominic clasped Arianna's shoulders and turned her to him. "The del Vecchio fortune began draining away long ago. The *marchesa's* father lost an enormous amount of money on a foolish venture in Naples. Her brother lost almost as much at the gaming tables in Monaco. And the *marchesa* only made things worse. She made bad investments, refused to listen to her advisors, and she's lived a certain life style. I suspect she refused to believe she could run out of funds."

"But she did." Arianna's voice broke. "And I made it worse by demanding money for the Butterfly."

"You had no way of knowing the true situation. But yes. She liquidated the last of her assets, took the loan from me and poured it all into the Butterfly."

Arianna made a little sound of distress and sank into a chair. Dominic squatted before her and cupped her chin. She tried to brush his hand away but he ignored her. He slid his hand around her neck and urged her head forward and she gave in to the gentle pressure and rested her forehead against his shoulder. He smelled of sunlight and soap and man, and she felt as if she could stay in his arms forever.

All the more reason to lift her head and free herself of his embrace.

"When she loses the Butterfly, she'll have nothing left. How will she live?"

A muscle knotted in his jaw. "She doesn't have to lose the Butterfly." He rose to his feet. "I never wanted it in the first place."

"You never…?" Arianna shook her head. "I don't understand. You accepted it as collateral."

"Your grandmother is an unusual woman." His smile softened his face. It made her think back to the first time they'd made love, the way he'd smiled afterward and left her wondering how many other women he'd looked at that same way. "Did she ever tell you how she managed to meet with me?"

"No. I mean, I assume she made an appointment."

"She bluffed her way past two reception areas to my assistant's desk, and refused to leave until she saw me. She said she needed six billion *lire*. I said I wasn't a bank. She talked some more and I said I'd give her the money. She was too proud to accept it."

Arianna laughed softly. "Yes. That sounds like… You said you'd *give* her the money?"

Dominic shrugged, as if embarrassed to admit to such weakness. "She refused."

"She'd have seen it as charity."

"Yes. So we agreed on a loan. And on the interest rate, which was more than I wished her to pay."

"And you checked on her finances after the fact?" Arianna lifted an eyebrow. "Not a very clever way to do business, *signore*."

"I checked because I sensed she was a woman in distress. And if you're hoping it's all a mistake, *cara*, it isn't. My people were thorough."

"I should have suspected something was wrong. I asked her why she was borrowing money instead of investing her own, and she said it was on the recommendation of her advisors."

"If she'd paid attention to them years ago," Dominic said wryly, "all this could have been prevented."

Arianna nodded. She thought about her grandmother, living her final years in poverty. No. She wouldn't let that happen. There had to be a way.

"My *nonna* is an old woman," she said softly. "She's in poor health. Once you take the Butterfly, what will become of her?"

Dominic tucked his hands into the back pockets of his jeans and paced the kitchen.

"Dominic?" She rose and went toward him. "Let me pay back the money she owes you."

He shook his head.

"I can do it. Four hundred dollars a month."

He shook his head again.

"Five hundred."

He smiled. Arianna didn't blame him. Five hundred dollars a month on six billion *lire*... Doing the math was pointless. At that rate, she'd never pay off the loan.

"Two thousand," she said desperately. "Six."

The Butterfly wasn't making enough money for that but she'd find a way to meet the debt. Take another job. Sell the pearls she'd inherited from her mother, the lovely old china...

"Please, Dominic. There has to be a way."

She was looking at him through lashes that glittered with tears, her mouth trembling. She had looked at him the same way that night in his bed as he'd moved between her thighs and opened her to him. It had almost stopped him, that look on her face, as if she feared him and his possession, but then she'd lifted her arms to him, drawn him down to her, down, down, down...

"I can help you," he said, and heard the simple words buzz in his head like the soft whisper of bees drawn to the sweet nectar of an exotic flower.

"How?"

"Have you forgotten, *cara?* I made you an offer and I'm still waiting for your answer."

She stared at him. He could tell that she really didn't know what he was talking about. Then the color drained from her face.

"No," she said sharply. "I won't do it."

"You mean, you don't want my help."

"You bastard! You arrogant, insufferable—"

He pulled her close against him and kissed her. She fought him and he clasped her face between his hands, held her still, held her mouth to his until he felt her start to tremble.

"Marry me," he said in a husky whisper, "and your grandmother's life will go on as it always has."

"That's blackmail!"

"It's a simple statement of fact."

"I won't sell myself to you."

"Is that how you see an arranged marriage that will benefit two families? How many del Vecchio brides have been 'sold' over the centuries, do you think?"

"My grandmother wouldn't want me to marry for money."

"For money. For the del Vecchio name to remain powerful. For an infusion of new blood." His eyes grew hot. "She wants an heir. So do I."

He already had an heir. The words almost burst from Arianna's throat. God, what was she doing to do?

"The terms of the agreement are simple, Arianna. I'll forgive the loan. I'll sign the Butterfly over to you, to save the *marchesa's* precious pride, and you can do what you wish with it. Keep it, give it back to her...the choice will be yours."

"What's the matter, *signore?*" Arianna jerked free of his hands. "Are you such a bad catch you have to buy yourself a wife?"

Dominic made a sound that was almost a laugh. "I'm a good catch, *cara.* And that's problem."

"Such modesty."

"Such honesty, you mean. It isn't easy for a man like me to find the right woman."

"Oh, I'll just bet it isn't."

"I'm sure the *marchesa* realized that when she suggested we'd make a good match. And I'm sure she expected me to court you. Take you out a few times, send you flowers…"

"Do you really expect me to believe any of this? My grandmother told me how the subject of marriage came up. That you suggested it."

Dominic's eyes narrowed. He checked his watch, then reached into his pocket and took out a cell phone.

"Your grandmother is probably in my car right now," he said coldly, "on her way to the airport." He flipped the phone open and held it toward her. "Press the second button. When my driver answers, ask to speak with her."

Silence filled the room. Arianna stared into Dominic's eyes. Was it true? Could her grandmother have made such a bizarre suggestion?

She shook her head, backed away from his outstretched hand as if it held a venomous insect instead of a phone.

"Even if it were true, why would you consider it? It's crazy."

"I thought so, too." Dominic slid the phone into his pocket. "And then I began considering the possibilities."

"What possibilities? If you want a wife, why should it be me?"

Why, indeed? He thought about the way she felt in his arms, how she trembled when he touched her, how he'd dreamed of her the past five years…

"There are other women. You could have your pick."

A quick smile flashed across his face. "A compliment, *cara*. How nice."

"Don't patronize me, Dominic! You know what I mean."

"I could have my pick because I have a lot of money," he said bluntly, "and that's the problem. I don't want a woman professing undying love when all she really wants is my checkbook."

"You're losing me here. Isn't your checkbook what you're offering me? Three million dollars of it, anyway?"

Arianna put her hands on her hips. Her breasts lifted, straining against the thin cotton of her shirt. Dominic felt his body stir. Yes, he thought, this was one of the reasons he'd marry her...but not the only one.

He moved so quickly that she had no time to sidestep, his hands clasping her elbows, lifting her to her toes until her face was level with his. "That's why your grandmother's scheme has merit. Everything would be in the open. We'd both know why you married me. No undying declarations of love. No lies. You get to secure her future. I get—"

"A wife who would hate you." Arianna's voice shook. "Who would despise you. Who would—"

"Marriage isn't about sentiment."

"Not in your world, maybe, but it is in mine."

"You're behaving like a child, Arianna, wanting life to be a fairy tale. We all do what we must to survive."

"I'm not for sale!" Arianna slapped her palms against his chest. "Let go of me, Dominic. I'd do anything for my grandmother—"

"But not this." His mouth thinned. "I was good enough to scratch an itch, but not to be seen with in daylight and certainly not to marry."

The room became silent. The soft buzz of insects outside the screen door and the ominous tick tick tick of the wall clock belonged to another world. Time was running out, for the *marchesa,* for her, for Jonathan.

"Please," she said, "please, leave now."

"Why are you so eager to get rid of me?" He lowered his head and she saw herself mirrored in his eyes. "Is this your weekend hideaway? Do you have a lover who meets you here? Is he a better lover than me?"

He cupped her face, forced her head back. He could see what he was doing to her, that she'd gone from rage to defiance to something worse. Despair? Fear? Fear, yes. *What are you doing?* he asked himself, even as he tugged the pins from her hair until it tumbled around her shoulders.

"Admit the truth," he said roughly. "Say that you want me."

"I don't. I don't—"

He kissed her, crushing her mouth with his, nipping hard at her bottom lip. She gave a sharp little cry and he started to let go of her, hating himself for his loss of control, for taking what she didn't want to give, but then she whispered his name and kissed him back, wrapped her arms around him as she had that night, sobbed when he slipped his hand under her shirt and cupped her breast...

The shattered screen door slammed against the frame.

"Get your hands off the lady, you son of a bitch," a man yelled.

"Don't you hurt my mommy," a child cried and that, more than the man's fury or the pain of small, sharp teeth sinking into his leg, stopped Dominic cold.

CHAPTER SIX

THE entire world had gone crazy.

Dominic didn't know what to do first, peel the kid off his leg, defend himself against the man coming at him, or tell Arianna that shouting "No, don't! Stop!" wasn't having the desired effect on either the kid or the man.

If anything, it seemed to be encouraging the attack.

He acted on instinct, shaking the boy off just as the man threw a wild left. Dominic danced back, but the guy was persistent and came at him with the left again. His reaction was instinctive. He slipped the punch and countered with an uppercut to the chin.

Arianna's defender blinked, stiffened, and went down like a fallen tree.

"Jeff," Arianna screamed, and the boy threw himself at Dominic again.

"Dio!" Dominic roared as the kid's teeth found their mark a second time. He grabbed the child by the scruff of the neck and held the windmilling boy at arm's length.

"Arianna! Do something with your piranha!"

Arianna, kneeling beside her fallen lover with his head in her lap, looked at Dominic as if he were the devil incarnate.

"You—you—" She jumped to her feet, grabbed her son and held him tightly against her while she whispered words of comfort and stroked his hair.

She should be stroking *my* hair, Dominic thought grimly. *He* was the one who'd been mauled. His leg felt as if it had been chewed by a pack of Chihuahuas.

The man on the floor groaned and sat up.

The child in Arianna's arms buried his face in her shoulder and wept.

Without question, Dominic thought, he must have stumbled into an asylum for the insane.

He ran his hands through his hair, tugged down his shirt and slapped his hands on his hips. None of it helped him make sense of whatever in hell was happening here, but he was starting to think even an army of psychiatrists wouldn't be clever enough to do that.

A child who addressed Arianna as "Mommy"? A man who leaped to her defense? Was the child hers? Was the man her husband? Her lover? Was she leading a secret life in this little house in the country? Not that he gave a damn. Asking her to marry him had been a stupid, spur-of-the-moment mistake.

The world was filled with women who'd jump at the chance to be his wife, women who didn't come equipped with sharp-toothed children and lovers who thought you'd been poaching on their territory—except how could you trespass on a man's rights to a woman when you hadn't even known he existed?

"It would seem," Dominic said coldly, "that there are some things your grandmother forgot to mention."

The child jerked his head around. "Don't you yell at my mother!"

"Hush, sweetheart." Arianna's tone was soft but the look she gave Dominic was poisonous. "She doesn't know."

Dominic stared at her. "Excuse me? You have a child, a husband—"

"He isn't my mom's husband," the boy said firmly. "'Cause if he were, I'd have a father. And I don't."

Arianna blinked. This was the first time Jonathan had ever mentioned having—or not having—a father. His timing couldn't have been worse.

"You don't need a father," she said, and hugged him closer. "You have me."

"That's what I told Jeff," the boy said tearfully, "when he asked if I wanted him for a dad."

"Oh, hell." Jeff got to his feet. "I didn't think Jonathan would say anything. Arianna…"

"Did you actually discuss this with my son?" Arianna said in disbelief.

"I figured I'd see how he felt about it," Jeff said unhappily, "before I approached you."

"Well, you shouldn't have. Whatever were you thinking?"

Jeff winced as he waggled his jaw from side to side. "I think that son of a bitch broke my jaw!"

"Watch your mouth," Dominic said sharply.

"And who in hell are you, anyway? Coming in here, attacking Arianna—"

"He wasn't attacking me. And he's right. Don't use language like that in front of Jonathan."

"Lotsa people say sum of a bitch," the child said helpfully. "They say other stuff, too, like—"

"Jonathan. Honey." Arianna's voice was bright. "Is Billy outside? Why don't you go play with him?"

"He doesn't feel good. We caught a fish and he threw up. That's why we came home."

"Oh. Oh, well then…why don't you go into the living room and put on the Saturday cartoons?"

"You don't let me watch the Saturday cartoons."

"Today's different."

"It surely is," Dominic said coldly. "I suspect it isn't every day you play hostess to your lover and a—how do you say it?—a patsy at the same time."

"What's a patsy, Mommy?"

"Hush, sweetheart!" Arianna glared at Dominic. "Have you no sense of decency? There's a child present!"

Dominic didn't answer. It was becoming difficult to be

civilized. The more time went by, the more he wondered what sort of woman would melt in one man's arms while she waited for another

"I was wondering when you'd get around to that."

"Not that it's any of your business, but Jeff isn't my... He's just a friend. And I don't know what you mean by a patsy."

"Oh, I think you do. At least now I understand the reason I was told none of this. You and the *marchesa* were afraid I wouldn't take the bait if I knew you had a child."

"Damn you, Dominic—"

"'Have you no sense of decency?'" he said, mimicking her. "'There's a child present'—a child I knew nothing about."

Arianna swallowed hard. "That isn't my fault. You came here thinking you knew everything about me. And—"

"And I didn't. As I pointed out, I was the perfect *pazzo*."

"I don't know what you mean!"

"It was clever, I admit." His mouth twisted. "You'd snag a husband and a fortune in one step. All you and the *marchesa* had to do was lure me in, make me think *I'd* been the one who'd maneuvered *you* into marriage...."

"Don't be crazy! It was nothing like that. Didn't I just tell you that the *marchesa* doesn't know about—about any of this? Maybe you should have asked me about my life instead of her!"

"What's he talking about?" Jeff put a hand against his jaw and winced again. "Who's the *marchesa?*"

"She's the matchmaker from hell," Dominic said coldly, his eyes never leaving Arianna's. "Do you really expect me to believe she knows nothing of this second life you lead?"

"You know what?" Fury made Arianna incautious. "I don't care what you believe. I just want you out of my house and my life."

"Finally, we agree."

Dominic started for the door. Arianna almost groaned with relief. Thank God! He was leaving, and he hadn't noticed Jonathan's resemblance to him. He'd go away and never come back. He'd be out of her life and her son's forever...

He'd go straight to her grandmother.

Of course he would. He didn't believe a word she'd said. He'd confront the *marchesa,* make these same accusations, talk about Jonathan...

Years of caution, of secrecy, of protecting her *nonna* from news she might not be well enough to handle, was all coming undone.

"Dominic!" She gave Jonathan a quick kiss and put him down. "Wait."

He turned to her. She saw the banked fury in his eyes and knew she had to be careful.

"We have to talk.

"We have nothing to talk about."

"Please. Just give me five minutes to take care of things here. You can wait on the back porch. It's quiet and peaceful."

Quiet and peaceful. As if he gave a damn about that. He'd been set up, used, manipulated...

"You'd be wasting your time." He folded his arms and glared at her. "There's no point in talking about the Butterfly, Arianna. I'm going to do what I should have done all along."

"I don't give a damn about the Butterfly! It's—it's—" She shot a quick look over her shoulder at the child and the man. "Please. Wait on the porch. Five minutes. Surely you can give me that."

Dominic scowled. Why should he give her anything? This woman couldn't seem to take an honest breath.

He looked past her. The man she claimed was not her lover stood behind the child, one hand on the boy's head in a protective gesture. At least he had good instincts. If anyone needed protection, it was the boy.

He was a brave little kid who'd defended his mother against huge odds. From the looks of him, he was ready to do it again. He looked small but undeniably fierce, his posture matching Dominic's right down to the narrowed eyes and folded arms.

Dominic cocked his head. Such perfect mimicry...

"Dominic?" Arianna put her hand on his arm. "I'm begging you. Please."

There was definite pleasure in hearing supplication in the voice of the princess.

"Five minutes," he said, as he moved past her. "Not a second more."

Half an hour later, Dominic was sitting on the porch steps, still waiting, still trying to figure out why he'd bothered to oblige Arianna by hanging around.

Whatever she had to say would only be more claptrap about her innocence in an unraveling scheme.

He didn't believe a word of it.

Twenty minutes ago he'd heard a door slam, a car engine start, a vehicle peel out of the driveway, its throaty roar a clear statement of dissatisfaction.

So much for Jeff of the glass jaw.

But Arianna hadn't appeared. He figured she was still soothing the boy.

And he was still hanging around. Well, why not? After all, it was a long time since anybody had tried to scam him.

Dominic leaned back on his elbows. Arianna was right. It was pleasant out here, as quiet as the countryside outside Rome. It was hot, too, the same as Rome, but flowering vines curled around the porch stanchions and offered patches of cooling shade.

A small bird with bright yellow feathers landed on the railing and scolded him for being there.

Dominic could hardly blame the bird. What *was* he doing here, except waiting to see just how far Arianna was prepared to go before she let the scam die a natural death?

He'd done a lot of scamming himself when he was a kid, conning tourists out of *lire* by claiming he was the best guide Rome had to offer, though half the time he'd passed off one old church or ruin by the name of another. Why not? he'd figured. Back then he had a righteous contempt for the rich.

Years later, he knew it hadn't been contempt at all. It had been envy.

Dominic sat up and let his hands dangle between his thighs.

A good sting called for a con artist with imagination. Arianna and the *marchesa* had as much as he'd ever seen. They'd set up a close-to-perfect con. Dangle a beautiful woman in front of a man who'd already tasted her favors, let her put on a don't-touch-me act while he could think of nothing but the night she'd spent in his bed, then make him feel so sorry for her that he'd give her anything she wanted.

Perfect, all right.

Too bad for the del Vecchios that the wheels had come off their plan. Timing was everything, and the timing on this had gone bad. The kid was supposed to stay out of sight just a little longer, probably until Arianna let herself be seduced into bed again.

He was sure now that she'd known who he was the night they'd been together. Forget all that nonsense about electricity sizzling between them. What had been sizzling was Arianna's clever scheme on the back burner....

A scheme so clever it had taken five years to pull off?

Dominic frowned.

That didn't make sense. There wasn't a take in the world worth such a long build-up. Yes, the pay-off was big, but five years?

Okay. Maybe she hadn't set him up that night. That

didn't mean that what was happening now hadn't been planned. The del Vecchio women saw their fortune gurgling down the drain, and he was their chance to get it back. The *marchesa* had dangled the bait. Arianna had set the hook with the marry a Martian routine...

Sighing, Dominic rose to his feet, tucked his hands in the back pockets of his khakis and went down the steps.

He could hardly wait to get home. What he'd told the *marchesa* about having business in New York wasn't true. The ''business'' had been Arianna. Now, he was eager to see Rome again.

Too bad he wasn't there right now, doing something simple like sitting at a café in the *piazza* near the Trevi fountain, drinking something tall and cool with Isabella or Antonia or any one of half a dozen other beautiful women who'd be happy to smile at him and say yes, without question they wanted the honor of being his wife.

At least he'd know, up front, if they had any surprises for him, like lovers tucked away in country houses no one knew existed...

Or children.

Saved by the skin of his teeth. Wasn't that what Americans said when you miraculously escaped a disaster? Imagine if Arianna had said yes, she'd marry him, and oh, by the way, had she mentioned she had a son?

Whose child was he? Dominic started down a narrow, foot worn path through the grass. Who had slept with Arianna and planted a seed in her womb?

Not that it mattered. After today, he'd never see her again. Anger, carnal desire, who knew what had been driving him? At least he'd come to his senses before it was too late.

What man would marry a woman he barely knew, business arrangement or not?

Dominic kicked a small stone out of the path.

The child was the final touch. A ready-made family, to start married life? He shook his head. No way.

Still, Arianna would make some man a good wife.

She was bright, she was beautiful, she was passionate. Not just in bed. In her work, too. He had to admit he liked that about her. If he'd married her, she'd have slipped seamlessly into his world, where money bought respect if not approbation, and if anyone had dared to look down on her because she was the wife of a man who'd come up from the streets, she'd have made short work of them.

Arianna was tough, like her grandmother. Maybe "strong" was a better word. It was an unusual quality in a woman who was beautiful. In his experience, beautiful women invariably acquiesced to men.

Not Arianna.

She'd apparently passed on that strength to the boy. Dominic laughed to himself. The way the kid had come at him, ready to take him... How old could the child be? Four? Five? He supposed he'd been pretty tough at that age, too, honed to steely resiliency by the streets.

If he ever had a son, he'd want him to be just like that. Confident. Sturdy. *If* he ever had a son...

Dominic caught his breath. The boy was just about the right age, but it couldn't be. He'd used condoms. He always did. He was always careful.

"Dominic?"

He turned and saw Arianna coming toward him. He met her halfway. She gasped with surprise as he grabbed her shoulders and hoisted her to her toes.

"Is he mine?"

Arianna's throat constricted, but she didn't bother pretending ignorance. She'd been preparing for this question while she'd dealt with Jeff, then put her son in for a nap and sat with him as he fell asleep. That was the only reason she could meet Dominic's hot gaze and lie through her teeth.

"No," she said calmly, "he's not."

Dominic's hands bit into her flesh. His expression was grim. Hers, she hoped, was neutral. When finally he let go of her and tucked his hands into his pockets, she breathed a silent "thank you" to the angel who'd surely been watching over her.

"Whose is he, then? Your friend with the bad left hook?"

Arianna shook her head. Was it cold out here, or was it her? She gave a little shudder and tucked her hands into the pockets of her shorts.

"I told you. Jeff is only a friend. Not even that. He's Jonathan's swimming coach. He has a son the same age and the boys like to spend time together."

"Were you widowed? Divorced? Who is the boy's father?"

"What is this, an interrogation?"

"It's a simple question."

"Here's a simple answer. I've never been married and Jonathan is mine. That's all you need to know."

"Jonathan. Quite a mouthful for a little kid. Don't you ever call him John or Johnny?"

"What I call him," Arianna said deliberately, "is none of your business."

"Be careful, *cara.*" Dominic flashed a warning smile. "A little while ago, you were pleading with me to stay so you could ask me a favor."

"I didn't say that."

"You didn't have to. It was obvious. So I stayed, and now you think you can insult me. That's not a good way to get whatever it is you want."

He was right, it wasn't. She just didn't want him asking questions about Jonathan. There were too many questions and not enough answers.

"I'm sorry."

He laughed. "The words came out as if they'd been stuck in your throat."

"Really, I *am* sorry. You're right. I asked you to stay and you did." Arianna glanced back at the house. Jonathan's room was upstairs. He probably wouldn't hear them, but she didn't want to risk it. "Let's walk a little further. The path leads into the pines."

Dominic shrugged. "As you wish."

She fell in beside him and they walked into the woods in silence. The tall pines shut out the sun, making the day seem suddenly cool, and she shuddered again.

"You're cold," Dominic said.

"I'm fine." She stopped walking and swung toward him. "I know you're—you're upset."

Dominic laughed and Arianna felt her cheeks redden.

"All right. You're more than upset. My grandmother made you think I'd be—that I'd be interested in marrying you. And now you seem to think she and I set you up."

"Go on." Dominic folded his arms. "Let's hear the rest of what you think."

"We didn't. I didn't, anyway. I didn't know who you were until yesterday, and I certainly have no wish to marry you." She paused. "Now you've stumbled across my—my hidden life."

"A truly bad title for a soap opera, *cara.*"

"But accurate." Arianna took a deep breath. "How did you find out about this house? I've kept its existence a secret."

"There are no secrets from a man who can afford to buy them."

"You called this place a love nest." A breeze blew a strand of her hair across her face. She caught it and tucked it behind her ear. "It's never been that. I bought it after my son was born." She paused. "It was the only way I could think of to keep his existence a secret."

"Because he is illegitimate?"

"Of course not! He's my son. I'm proud of him. I love him with all my heart."

"But he has no father." Dominic's mouth thinned. "A child should not be held responsible for the errors of its parents. If his father didn't want to acknowledge him—"

"Jonathan's father doesn't know he exists. I wanted it that way. We had—we had only a brief relationship."

"A man is entitled to know he's sired a child, and a child is entitled to know his father."

"Dammit, don't preach to me, Dominic! That's easy for you to say, but you don't…" Arianna fought for composure. "The issue here is not my son's birth. It's the choices I made after it. There was no reason for the man involved ever to know about my child."

Arianna shuddered again. Dominic muttered an oath, ignored her protests as he wrapped his arm around her and drew her into the warmth of his body.

"And the *marchesa?* Surely she would be happy to know she has a grandson."

"The *marchesa* lives in a world that doesn't exist." Arianna looked up at him. "She still believes in white gloves, and servants, and calling cards, and—"

"And babies who are never born out of wedlock."

Arianna nodded as they turned and began walking out of the pine woods.

"Exactly. Still, I was going to tell her…but she had a heart attack. How could I give her such news when she was ill? So I waited. And waited. And the more time passed, the more difficult it became. I'd look at her and see the evidence of the years etched into her face, or she'd talk scornfully of some new medical test she'd had…"

"Time moves on."

"Yes."

"All the more reason for her to want to see you married. She wants to insure the future of the del Vecchios."

Dominic paused. "As I wish to insure the future of the Borgheses."

He spoke softly, so softly that it was almost a whisper. Arianna was afraid to look at him, but he stopped walking and turned her to him. "I think your grandmother knows that, and hoped I'd find her suggestion not quite as outlandish as it might seem."

"You don't have to apologize for her. And I'm glad you admit it was outlandish."

Dominic lay his fingers lightly across Arianna's mouth.

"I did, at first. But then—I'm not sure when, but at some point, it began to make a strange kind of sense." His voice turned husky. "I would get a beautiful princess for my wife, she would keep her precious Butterfly, and someday there would be a Borghese-del Vecchio heir."

"Dominic—"

"But," he said, tilting her face to his, "I misjudged the beautiful princess. She doesn't want any of that badly enough to pawn her soul to the devil."

"You're not—"

"Hush." There were tears on Arianna's lashes. Gently, he wiped them away with his thumb. "It's all right, *cara.* There are better ways to find a wife than to fall into a game devised by a sly old woman." He slid his hands into her hair. "It could have worked, you know. Do you remember that night? You and I...we made the earth tremble."

Arianna met his eyes. She had lied to him about the one thing that mattered more than anything else in the world. How could she lie to him about this, too?

"Yes. We did." Her voice shook. "I want you to know something, Dominic. I never—never in my entire life... what I felt that night, what you made me feel..."

He bent to her and kissed her, softly at first, then with growing hunger. She leaned into his embrace, her mouth open to his, her heart beating fast with the excitement of being in his arms again.

"Arianna." He pulled back enough so he could look into her eyes, forgot what he'd told himself about not wanting this woman, forgot even that he didn't want a child another man had given her. "*Bellisima* Arianna, let's start over. Let's pretend we only just met. We'll go to dinner. To the theater. We'll walk in the park. Whatever pleases you…"

"Mommy?"

They jumped apart, torn from each other's arms by the sound of that small, uncertain voice. Jonathan was standing on the porch steps, hair tousled, feet bare, a well-loved teddy bear clutched in his arms.

"Yes, sweetheart." Arianna tried to read her son's face. What had he seen? What had he heard? She went to him and held out her arms, but he took a step back. "Did you have a bad dream?"

"He's still here," her son said, staring at Dominic. "That man you said had to leave."

She looked back at Dominic. "He is leaving," she said quickly. "Right now."

Dominic shook his head. "Not yet." His tone was easy, his smile warm. He walked to the porch, squatted down when he reached the steps and held out his hand. "I think it's time we met properly, Jonathan. My name is Dominic."

Arianna held her breath. Her son stared steadfastly at this stranger. Then, slowly, he stuck out his hand and let it be engulfed by Dominic's.

"I never heard that name before."

"It's Italian."

"I know about Italy. They play soccer there."

Dominic nodded gravely. "Indeed they do, only we call it football."

"Jeff was gonna take me to a football game in the fall."

"Was he," Dominic said coolly.

"Do you have a little boy at home, like Jeff does?"

"I wish I did, but I don't."

"And do you want to marry my mommy, like Jeff does?"

"Jonathan," Arianna said quickly, but Dominic's voice cut across hers.

"What would you think if I did?"

"Dominic!" Arianna reached for her child and hoisted him into her arms. "Jonathan, you don't have to worry about me marrying anybody. I'd never—"

"I think you should marry somebody, Mommy. You don't know anything about stuff like football or soccer."

"Honey, we can talk about this another—"

"You could marry Dom—Dom—"

"Dominic," Dominic said helpfully.

"Dom'nic. 'Cause sometimes I think it would be nice to have a daddy, 'cept not one who gets knocked out so fast, like Jeff."

Dominic snorted. Arianna glared at him, then buried her face in her child's neck. "Jonathan," she whispered, "sweetheart, this isn't the time to—"

"That was a really good punch!"

Oh God. Her son sounded gleeful. "Jonathan," Arianna said firmly, "stop it right now."

"Just one kapow," Jonathan said, slapping his hands together so that the teddy bear swung in a wild arc, "and bam! Out ol' Jeff went."

Arianna put him down. "Listen to me, Jonathan."

"Gianni."

She stared at Dominic, who was exchanging man-to-man smiles with her son. "What did you call him?"

"Gianni. That's Italian for Johnny."

"I know what it means." The porch felt as if it were swaying under her feet. Arianna wrapped her hand around a stanchion. "But his name is Jonathan, not Johnny. Really, Dominic, don't you have an appointment back in the city?"

"He looks more like a Gianni than a Jonathan to me."

"Yeah, Mom. I look more like a Gianni than a Jonathan." The child made a face. "What do you call that? A nickname?"

Dominic smiled. *"Si."*

"That word's Italian, too. Right?"

"Right. It means yes."

"I always wanted a nickname, but my mom just calls me Jonathan." The child turned an innocent face to Arianna. "How come you never gave me a nickname?"

Arianna gave up. "You never asked," she said, and plopped down on the top step. She'd just have to ride out whatever was happening here.

"So, how come you were kissing my mother, Dom'nic?"

Arianna shook her head, then buried her face in her hands.

"Well, I like to kiss her." Dominic sat down, too, and pulled the boy into his lap. "Your mother is pretty."

"She's smart, too." Jonathan's voice filled with pride. "She runs a big store. In Manhattan. Do you know where Manhattan is?"

"Yes," Dominic said solemnly, "I do."

"I went to the park there once."

"Uh huh."

"An' to a museum."

"Jonathan." Arianna rose slowly to her feet. "That's enough. Say goodbye to Signore Borghese and go into the house."

"I thought his name was Dom'nic."

"It is," Dominic said. He stood up. *"Signore* means mister. And Borghese is my last name."

"Oh."

Oh, Arianna thought, while the hysteria mounted inside her, *oh?* Her son and his father were discussing names and sports and her—*her*—as if they were old pals.

This was a bad dream. It had to be. Maybe if she tried very hard, she'd wake up.

"Dominic." She took a deep breath. "Thank you for waiting. So we could talk, I mean. And thank you for being so understanding."

"You're welcome."

"I didn't expect…" Arianna put her hand on her son's head. "I thought it might take longer to convince you that, well, that… You know."

"Not to discuss today's events elsewhere?" He shrugged. "The timing of that matter is in your hands, not mine."

"Thank you. Let me just get Jonathan inside and I'll walk you to your—"

"Not that you have all that much time to deal with it."

"I know." She smiled as the tension inside her eased. Dominic Borghese wasn't a beast after all. He'd given her a bad few minutes, well, a bad couple of hours, but obviously he understood that he couldn't tell the *marchesa* about her son any more than she could marry him. "I'm going to talk to the *marchesa* this week. I'll fly to Florence and—"

"Tomorrow," Dominic said.

Arianna blinked. "Sorry?"

"I said, you'll fly to Florence tomorrow." He frowned. "My plane's probably left already, but I'm sure my office can arrange for airline tickets on short notice." He looked down at Jonathan and smiled. "Have you ever been to Italy, Gianni?"

"His name is Jonathan," Arianna said sharply. She took a step back, tugging her son with her. "What are you talking about? He's not going to Italy. Neither am I."

Dominic's eyes met hers. He was still smiling, but the steel in that smile sent a chill down her spine.

"I've agreed to permit you your own timing with regard

to telling your grandmother what must be told to her. As for the rest...I told you what I want of you, Arianna.''

She was speechless. ''You can't mean... You don't really think...''

''I do mean. I do think.''

''No! I'd never—''

''Think before you speak, *cara*. There's a great deal at stake here. Your grandmother's finances. The future of the Butterfly.'' Dominic paused. ''Your secret.''

''But you said—you said you wouldn't—''

''Mommy?''

''Hush, Jonathan.''

''Mommy!''

''Jonathan, please. This doesn't concern you. Why don't you go into the house? See if—if there's any popcorn. I'll be in and—''

''Mom-my,'' Jonathan said impatiently, ''who's that lady?''

''What la...'' Arianna looked across the yard. A moan burst from her throat. ''Oh God,'' she whispered, ''no. Please, no!''

Dominic's eyes followed hers. The *marchesa* was walking toward them, looking down at the uneven ground and leaning heavily on her walking stick as she picked her way through the grass. Dominic's driver was a couple of paces behind her, looking sheepish.

Dominic slid his arm around Arianna's waist and laid his hand on Jonathan's shoulder. He could feel Arianna trembling. He drew her closer, clasped the boy more tightly.

''Marchesa,'' he said politely, ''what a surprise.''

''Your plane was being serviced, Signore Borghese. Some nonsense about an engine, your pilot said. I had already given up my suite at the hotel and there I was, all alone. No host. No granddaughter. What was I to do? I phoned your apartment but there was no answer, and your driver was most reluctant to give me any information until

I…'' The old woman's eyes rounded. For the first time, she seemed to notice Jonathan. Her face turned a papery white.

"Arianna? Who is this child?"

"Mommy?" Jonathan looked up at Arianna. "Mommy, why is the lady such a funny color?"

The *marchesa's* mouth dropped open. "What did the boy call you?"

"Nonna." Arianna broke away from Dominic and ran down the steps. *"Nonna,* let me help you. Come and sit down."

"I want answers, Arianna! Who is this boy?"

"I'm Jonathan Cabot. Who are you?"

"Dio." The *marchesa* whispered the word like a prayer. She put her hand to her throat just as Arianna's arm curled around her waist. "Arianna, tell me it isn't so."

"Please, grandmother…"

"Tell me the boy isn't yours."

"I *am,* too, hers! Tell her, Mommy."

Jonathan sounded brave but he leaned back against Dominic's legs and Dominic could feel him shake. He cursed under his breath and lifted the child into his arms, remembering all too clearly the pain of a childhood spent in the shadows.

"Signore Borghese?" The *marchesa* stamped her walking stick on the grass, but with far less force than usual. "Explain this immediately."

"I'll explain," Arianna said quickly. "I just don't know where to start."

"You don't have to, *cara.*"

Dominic spoke softly, but there was no mistaking the air of quiet command in his voice as he came down the steps, holding Jonathan in one arm, and stood close beside Arianna.

"Do you recall when your granddaughter and I confessed that we had known each other in the past?"

"A brief meeting, you said. At a party."

"It's true. We did meet at a party."

Dominic smiled at Arianna. At least, she thought, it would look like a smile to her grandmother but what she read in his eyes was a warning.

"The truth is that we had more of a relationship than we admitted. And now we have some news that should please you."

"No," Arianna said breathlessly, "Dominic..."

It was too late. Dominic drew her into the curve of his arm.

"Your granddaughter and I are getting married."

CHAPTER SEVEN

THEY were married in the Manhattan chambers of a judge Dominic knew. The ceremony was brief and the only guests were the *marchesa* and Gianni.

Dominic had to keep reminding himself Arianna didn't want him to use that name. Her son's name was Jonathan, she said emphatically, just before the ceremony began. He was American, not Italian. She wanted Dominic to remember that.

The boy looked so crestfallen that Dominic came close to telling her he'd call the child by whatever name he wished, but he knew there were times it was best to let things ride.

"Let's not quarrel," he said pleasantly. "What's the importance of a name, anyway?"

Arianna didn't answer. She didn't have to. He knew that they were jockeying for position, establishing the rules for a marriage neither of them had planned. It was logical, though. For a man in his position and a woman in hers, an arranged marriage made sense.

That was what Dominic told himself, anyway. But when he stood beside Arianna as the judge spoke, when he felt her tremble, when he reached for her hand and she looked up at him as if he had the answers to all the questions in the universe, he found himself suddenly wondering if perhaps he was marrying her for some other reason.

There was no time to think about it.

"By the power vested in me by the State of New York..." the judge said and just that quickly, the ceremony—and the moment—were over.

The judge smiled. "Congratulations."

Dominic nodded. ''Thank you.''

''Well? Aren't you going to kiss the bride?''

Dominic turned to Arianna, prepared to offer nothing more than a *pro forma* brush of his lips against hers, but she turned her head to the side and his kiss landed on her cheek.

It made him angry.

Did she think the touch of his mouth would be some sort of contaminant? Was she too good to accept a kiss from a peasant? He wanted to grab her and force a real kiss on her, twist his hand in her hair and hold her still under the pressure of his mouth until she moaned and kissed him back.

But he controlled himself.

He was overreacting. This was difficult for Arianna. Everything had happened very quickly. Their arrangement, the ceremony, the *marchesa* learning about Jonathan— news the old woman had received with surprising good grace, just as he'd hoped, because she believed the boy was his—all of it had taken place in the blink of an eye.

He understood that his new wife needed time to adapt.

In fact, he decided to tell her that.

They had lunch at a restaurant in the east sixties. Dominic ordered vintage champagne and the *marchesa* offered a toast.

''To the future of our new *famiglia*.''

Dominic drank. So did the *marchesa*. Smiling, she offered her glass to her newly found great-grandson and even Jonathan swallowed a drop of the pale golden wine.

Arianna raised her glass to her lips but that was all. She didn't drink, didn't smile, didn't acknowledge Dominic's presence.

''Are you okay, Mommy?'' Jonathan asked, and she smiled then and said yes, she was fine, just a little tired, but Dominic knew it was a lie.

She was upset, that was all. There was still confusion in her eyes....

Or was it hate?

That evening, after they'd boarded his jet and both the *marchesa* and Jonathan were asleep, he slipped into the seat beside Arianna's and took her hand.

"I know this was very sudden," he said, "and that, perhaps, you have not yet adjusted to this change in your life...."

He got no further. She pulled her hand from his and looked at him through eyes so flat they might have been made of glass.

"Don't touch me!"

"Arianna..."

"You forced me into this marriage. Did you think I'd forgive you for that?"

"Your grandmother—"

"Don't blame it on her! And don't change the facts. You'd already announced that I was marrying you before my grandmother put a foot out of that car."

Stung, Dominic fired back.

"Excuse me, *cara*, but I don't see any chains on your wrists. You stood before the judge willingly this morning."

"Willingly? I was as trapped as—as a pawn in some medieval power play."

"You could have said no."

"And shatter my *nonna's* health and dreams?" Arianna shook her head. "You know better than that."

"Let me be sure I understand this. Because you wanted to protect the *marchesa* and because I provided a way out, because you chose to go along with the fiction I'd created right up to letting me put a wedding ring on your finger...because of those things, I'm the villain and you're the martyr. Is that it?"

Her face reddened. Seeing it gave him grim pleasure.

"You're twisting my words! That's not what I meant."

"No?" Dominic flashed a tight smile. "Then perhaps you'll tell me what you *did* mean."

"You were the one who wanted an arranged marriage. Now you have one. Don't blame me if you don't like what you got."

"That's not an answer."

"It's the only one you're going to get."

Dio, he wanted to... What? Slap her? Never. He wasn't a man who'd hit a woman, no matter how she treated him. He could shake her instead, or rave and rant...or haul her against him and kiss her until she had to acknowledge the truth, that they could make an arranged marriage work.

No, he wouldn't do that. He was angry, but he wasn't a fool.

"It's time we agreed to something, Arianna."

"What could we possibly agree to, except that this was a mistake?"

"One thing," he snapped, doing his best to hang on to his temper. "You will treat me with respect at all times."

"Fine. I can manage that, as long as you agree to the one thing I require." She waited for him to give her his full attention. "Don't even think of trying to sleep with me."

Oh, the sheer pleasure of seeing the shock in his eyes. He looked at her as if she'd spoken in an unknown language.

"I beg your pardon?"

"I said, I won't share your bed. You want me to make it clearer? We're not going to have sex, Dominic."

"We will."

"We won't. It's not up for discussion."

"You're right. It isn't." He leaned close, clasped her wrist and brought her hand up between them. She was putting his temper to an impossible test! "We are man and wife."

"Husband and wife." The tilt of her chin defied him not

to recognize the difference. "That doesn't give you the right to my body."

"What are you hoping? That I'll tell you I'll divorce you if you demand a sexless marriage?" His voice roughened. "Or that I'll force you into my bed to do what we both know you want?"

"Are you threatening me?"

"You are my wife." He dropped her wrist and sat back, afraid of what he might do if she went on provoking him. "I'll give you some time to begin behaving like one, but I warn you, I'm not a patient man."

He got up and walked away. She plucked a magazine from a low table, snapped it open and buried her nose in its glossy pages as if she were actually reading it. As if she could. As if she could think of anything except what Dominic had referred to as this change in her life.

Change? He'd turned her world inside out. Did he really think he could do such a thing and get away with it?

He damn well couldn't and the sooner he understood that, the better.

Arianna kept the magazine in front of her face until the plane touched down at Ciampino Airport. Then she reached for Jonathan.

"Say goodbye to your grandmother," Dominic said gruffly. "I'll get the boy."

"The *boy*," she said coldly, "is my son. I'll carry him."

"Do as you're told."

He brushed past her and carried the sleeping child to the chauffeured car that was waiting for them. *Dio,* he was furious! Did Arianna think she could treat him this way and get away with it? Did she think she could benefit by this marriage but go on pretending he'd forced her into it? By the time she joined him a few minutes later, Dominic was seething.

The car began moving and he pressed the button that raised the privacy partition.

Arianna reached for the child again. "I'll take him now."

"Gianni is exhausted. Let him sleep."

"His name is Jonathan. I keep telling you that. And he can sleep quite comfortably in my lap."

Dominic felt the anger inside him swelling until it seemed lodged in the middle of his chest.

"Find something else to argue over, Arianna. I'm not going to let you use the boy."

"*Use* him? Perhaps you've forgotten. He's my son."

She spoke the words quickly, almost defiantly, as if to establish her rights. And she did have rights, Dominic knew. Far better rights than his. She was Gianni's mother. He was, at best, a stepfather who'd only laid eyes on the boy a handful of days ago.

Still, he felt protective of the kid and determined not to let Arianna poison the boy's feelings for him.

After a moment, Arianna turned and stared out the window as the car swept through the dark streets of the city. When it began to slow as they approached the Spanish Steps, she swung toward him again.

"I assume you have a guest room. Be sure and tell your chauffeur to put my things there."

"Is that how it's done in the United States? Wives and husbands have their own rooms?"

"This is not the United States, and I am not, in any meaningful sense of the word, your wife. I expect—"

"I know what you expect," he said brusquely. "You've made it clear. And I've decided to accommodate you. I shall have my quarters. You'll have yours. In business, I take what I want. On a personal level, I never take what isn't offered to me."

The car pulled to the curb. In the headlights of an oncoming vehicle, he saw color climb into her face again.

"Remember that," she said, as if he were a street urchin who needed lessons in behavior, and he felt such rage that he'd have swept her into his arms, carried her into the house and to his bed if Gianni hadn't been present.

No. Dammit, no. He wasn't going to let her reduce him to that level.

Instead, he grabbed her wrist. She gasped and he knew he was hurting her, but at that moment, he didn't give a damn.

"You'll have to beg me to take you to my bed. Do you understand, Arianna? As far as I'm concerned…"

The door swung open. He looked up and saw the chauffeur standing outside the car, heels together, spine straight, looking like a soldier at attention.

"Signore?"

The only thing missing was a salute. Dominic recognized the driver as a new man and started to tell him that he could forget about all that obsequious nonsense, that he despised being treated as if he were an emperor, but Arianna made a sound that might have been a little snort of derision.

Damn her to hell, he thought, and stepped from the car.

Three days later, he decided to make a small gesture of peace. They were living under one roof, sharing mealtimes for the boy's sake, but otherwise behaving like strangers.

No one could go on living this way.

They'd both said some rough things that first night, but it was understandable. He'd been tired. So had Arianna. Add in the shock of the marriage and jet lag, and you had a situation primed for disaster.

So he came to breakfast Saturday morning dressed in light canvas trousers and a navy T-shirt. Arianna and Gianni were already there.

"Good morning."

Arianna didn't respond. The boy looked up and grinned.

"Good morning, Dom'nic."

He smiled back and ruffled the kid's hair.

"I've been thinking…how would you like to see Rome?"

Gianni's eyes lit. "Cool! Mom? Dom'nic says—"

"I heard him." Arianna took a roll from the bread basket, broke it in pieces and began buttering it. She didn't look up. "I've seen Rome dozens of times."

"I haven't." Gianni had a hopeful expression on his face. "The only thing I saw was that big fountain the other day, when you and I went for a walk."

"Eat your eggs, please, Jonathan."

Dominic heard the edge in his wife's voice and decided to ignore it.

"Neither of you has seen *my* Rome," he said pleasantly. "There's a wonderful little church that's far off the tourist track, and a small garden with what's rumored to be a statue by Michelangelo inside. And I know a restaurant in the Jewish Quarter where they serve the most incredible fried artichokes."

"I don't like artichokes," Arianna replied, in a tone meant to end all discussion. "Jonathan, didn't I tell you to eat your eggs?"

"*I* like ardachopes," the boy said eagerly.

"You don't even know what they are. And you wouldn't like them."

"I bet he would." Dominic rose from the table, snatched Gianni up and swung him in the air. The kid liked that. It always made him giggle. "How about it, *compagno?* Want to go sightseeing with me today?" He held the boy at arm's length and dropped his voice to a whisper. "We'll go to the catacombs and see all the skulls and skeletons. How's that sound?"

"It's too hot for that," Arianna said quickly.

"Don't be silly. The catacombs are underground. It's probably 20 degrees cooler down there. Sound good to you, Gianni?"

"His name is—"

"Oh, yeah," Gianni said happily.

Dominic tucked him under his arm as if he were a football. The boy giggled even harder.

"We'll be home by dinnertime."

Arianna flashed him a look that could have frozen the Medusa, but he didn't care. He headed for the door without looking back. Maybe she didn't want to be his wife, but Gianni wanted to be his son.

His stepson.

This was his city. If his wife didn't want to share it with him, the boy did.

The day was filled with fun, but the smile on Gianni's face disappeared when they got back and found Arianna waiting. Dominic felt his own good mood fading. There was no mistaking her look of tightly banked rage.

"Go to your room," she told her son. The boy's lip trembled, and her expression softened. "I'm not angry at you, sweetheart."

"Don't be angry at Dom'nic, either. We had a really good time, Mom."

For a moment, Dominic thought she'd relent. Then she looked at him and her eyes hardened.

"Go to your room, please, Jonathan." As soon as he was gone, Arianna rounded on Dominic. "You will not undermine my authority again. I'm Jonathan's mother. I'll decide what he does and doesn't do."

Maybe if she'd suggested discussing things, Dominic would have reacted differently. But he was tired of her coldness, her rudeness, her dismissive attitude.

"You have it wrong. It is you who will not undermine *my* authority. This is my home. You are my wife. Gianni—Jonathan—may not be my natural son, but he is my responsibility now. I don't have to ask your permission for anything."

There was a quick flash of something in her eyes. Despair? Pain? Whatever it was, he sensed that it cut much deeper than his words. She turned away from him and left the room.

Dominic listened to the tap of her heels against the marble floor, heard the snick of the door to the guest suite as it shut behind her.

For a moment, he regretted his angry words. Then he thought of how she'd treated him since they'd exchanged their vows and decided he didn't regret anything....

Except, perhaps, the marriage.

A month later, nothing had changed.

It was a blisteringly hot August afternoon. The air conditioning in Dominic's office was having trouble keeping up with the heat. Maybe that was why he put down his pen, stared blindly out the window and finally faced the truth.

His marriage wasn't working.

He'd really believed that a marriage based on expedience *would* work. There'd be no need for lies or fairy tales.

He was wrong.

Knowing your wife had married you for reasons that had nothing to do with her heart was no better than suspecting it. In fact, it was worse. Had he married a woman who professed to love him, he might have been able to delude himself into believing it.

He'd have laughed if anyone had told him he wanted to come home at night to a kiss, to look up from reading the paper after dinner and see a smile meant only for him. The truth was—and it was almost painful to acknowledge—he wanted the little signs of affection that went with marriage, even if they were phony.

Dominic leaned his elbows on his desk and put his head in his hands.

He'd lived alone almost his entire life, but he'd never felt lonely until now. Part of it came from little things, like hearing his wife's laughter as he came to the front door...and hearing it stop, once he put his key in the lock.

Part of it came from her treating him as if he were a barbarian at the gate. She jumped if he brushed her arm as he moved past her in a narrow space, and sometimes he caught her looking at him with an expression that suggested she expected the worst of him at any minute.

He wasn't a monster. He wasn't going to demand she spend her evenings talking to him, instead of going to her room after Gianni was tucked in. He wasn't going to order her to his bed, despite his earlier threats. Why did she look at him that way? Why did she catch her breath if he came too close?

She was driving him crazy.

Was it deliberate? Did she know what she was doing? Had she really only wanted him when he was a stranger?

Heaven knew she wanted no part of him now that he was her husband.

Especially because he was her husband.

Dominic sat up straight. His wife was right about one thing. He'd forced her into this marriage. He might not admit it to her, but why lie to himself? And he'd be damned if he'd let her force him to end it. Maybe that was her plan, to make him unhappy enough to tell her all right, he'd had enough, it was over.

He wasn't going to do it.

Frowning, he picked up his pen and looked at the stack of letters awaiting his signature.

"See if you can't manage to sign them before the day ends," Celia had said, "and before you snap at me and tell me to mind my own business the way you've been doing lately, Signore Borghese, kindly remember that getting your letters out *is* my business."

It was a surprisingly blunt remark, even from his gorgon. Dominic had lifted his eyebrows, but he'd said nothing. He knew he deserved the chastisement.

He'd been staring at the letters for two days and the only thing that had changed was that the stack had grown higher.

He didn't actually have to read the mail. Celia was efficient. She typed his correspondence precisely as he dictated it, and in those instances where he told her to answer a letter herself, she always did so in ways he approved.

He wondered if she'd approve of the fact that he was married. He hadn't told anyone yet, except for his household staff. Why would you tell people you had a wife when, for all intents and purposes, you didn't?

Celia knew something was up, though. *Was he feeling all right?* she'd asked a couple of days ago. Certainly, he'd replied...but he suspected she hadn't bought the quick answer. He knew he wasn't behaving normally. Until a few weeks ago, he'd prided himself on being aware of everything that went on in his office.

He was the man in charge of what some called an empire.

How could you run an empire unless you had your head on your shoulders?

Dominic frowned.

It was a stupid metaphor and, lately, an even worse description of the job he was doing. His head wasn't on anything but his disastrous marriage.

His frown deepened. He plucked the first letter from the pile and stared at it.

Dear Carl, blah blah blah, as I explained when you telephoned, your plans for expanding Adrian International sound most promising, but unfortunately...

But, unfortunately, he really didn't give a damn about Adrian International.

Dominic cursed softly, dropped the letter and ran his hands over his face.

This had to stop.

He wasn't sleeping well at night, wasn't paying enough attention to work during the day, and he waffled when he made decisions. He'd always been a man who thought about what he was going to do and then did it, no regrets, no second-guessing, no time wasted on "what-if."

"Dominic Borghese runs his various enterprises with a firm hand and an enviable sense of conviction," a TV reporter in Milan had said of him recently. "Borghese researches an issue thoroughly before reaching a conclusion. As a result, he rarely needs to alter his position. If he does, you can count on something vital having changed in the equation."

Dominic tilted back his chair.

Really? What was the "something vital" that had changed his decision about marriage? He'd not only laughed at the idea of asking Arianna to be his wife, he'd laughed at the idea of asking anyone.

His long term plans had included a wife, but not now. And the wife he'd envisioned had been nothing like Arianna. What man would be foolish enough to choose a woman who was contrary? Who treated him with scorn?

Who'd borne another man a child?

That was another problem. He loved the boy more each day—who wouldn't? The kid was terrific. But he didn't like thinking about the faceless man who was Gianni's father. Arianna wouldn't talk about him at all, even though Dominic assured her he could accept that she had a sexual past. This wasn't the middle ages and trembling virgins weren't his style.

Then, why did it trouble him to know that some stranger had impregnated his wife? Why did he sometimes look at the boy and think how wonderful it would be if the kid could have been his?

The boy was the best thing, the only good thing, in this farce of a marriage.

Dominic went to a small refrigerator built into the wall, took out a bottle of mineral water and poured a glass.

Gianni was an amazing little boy. He was sweet-natured, he had a great sense of humor, and he showed an avid curiosity about everything…including the sleeping arrangements of his mother and stepfather.

''Aren't husbands and wives s'posed to sleep in the same room?'' he'd asked Dominic as they walked to a *gelato* shop a couple of days ago.

''Not necessarily,'' Dominic had said calmly, lying through his teeth. Of course husbands and wives were supposed to sleep in the same room, but he wasn't about to tell that to a little boy.

He wasn't about to tell it to Arianna, either.

He would not order his wife to his bed, though he had to admit he thought about it.

Thought about it, a lot.

No. He wouldn't do that.

Dominic's hand tightened on the water glass.

Instead, he would let his work slip, snap at Celia, drive his Ferrari so fast he'd been warned to slow down by a *politiziotto* that very morning—a thing virtually unheard of in a city where people drove as if they were on the course at Le Mans.

He'd do everything, including keep his promise about the Butterfly, which his attorneys were transferring to his wife's name.

Would she smile when he handed her the papers? Would she be happy to hear the amount of money he intended to put into the resurrection of the Butterfly?

Dominic lifted the glass to his lips and drank down the rest of the water, though he knew it would do nothing to cool his growing temper.

He knew the answers to his questions, too.

Arianna wouldn't show pleasure in anything, not if it involved him.

And that took him full circle, to the realization that since his wedding, he seemed willing to do anything…except deal with reality. He had a wife who was not a wife, and he was permitting it to happen.

The glass shattered under the pressure of his hand. He cursed, dumped the shards in the wastebasket and flung open the door to his office.

Celia looked up, clearly startled.

"Those letters on my desk?" he said as he strode past her. "Sign my name to all of them."

Celia stared at him as if she'd never seen him before. Was it because of what he'd said, or because he looked as furious as he felt? He didn't know. He didn't care. Nothing mattered except teaching his wife that she *was* his wife, and he was tired of pretending she wasn't.

Every man had his breaking point, and Dominic had reached his.

CHAPTER EIGHT

ARIANNA sat in a lounge chair on the terrace off the sitting room of Dominic's apartment, drinking an iced cappuccino as if she hadn't a care in the world.

One story below, in a flower-laced courtyard that looked as if it had come straight out of some glorious painting by Raphael, her little boy and his newfound best pal, Bruno, sprawled beneath a flowering tree, lying on their bellies as they played with a fleet of small wooden cars. On a terrace across the courtyard, a fat Persian cat basked contentedly in the sun.

It was a beautiful, peaceful scene in stark, almost brutal contrast to the despair in Arianna's heart.

A month had gone by since Dominic had forced her into marriage and brought her here, a month since she'd become his unwilling wife…and a month that she'd awakened each morning, terrified that it would be the day he looked at the child he called his stepson and realized that Jonathan was his, and all her lies had been for nothing.

Her life, which had seemed so complicated in the States, had taken on enough added twists and turns so that her former existence seemed simple by comparison.

In America, she'd run a business without capital and raised a child without anyone knowing it.

In Italy, she spent endless days doing nothing and raised her child in the home of the man who'd fathered him, living in fear of the day he stopped believing that child had been fathered by someone else.

Arianna put down her glass of coffee and touched her fingers to her forehead, where the beginnings of a headache threatened.

The situation was so ludicrous that she'd probably laugh if she clicked on the TV and saw the same story unfold in an afternoon soap, but this wasn't a soap. It was her life, it was real, and she sometimes felt as if she were dancing on the edge of a razor.

Maybe if she had something to do, something to fill the endless hours…

But she didn't.

She knew now that Dominic's talk about handing over the Butterfly had been meant to placate her, nothing more. He'd kept his promise to the *marchesa* and not foreclosed on the business, but all the rest had turned to dust. He hadn't given it to Arianna to run, hadn't put his people to work on finding ways to improve its financial health, hadn't even mentioned it again except to say once, in passing, that he'd sent in a team to inventory the stock.

Arianna hissed, closed her eyes and pressed her hand against her head.

The headache had arrived, as promised. No surprise there. The one thing she could count on, every day, was that her head would pound. Tension, stress… Sometimes, she felt like an advertisement for aspirin.

Had Dominic told her about the inventory just to bait her? Maybe he'd figured she'd say, *What happens when your people are finished? Will you keep your promise and let me take over again?*

If that's what he hoped, he was in for a disappointment. She'd never ask him for anything, never tell him she wanted anything, never let him see her beg.

God, how she hated her husband!

"Mommy? Hey, Mom!"

Arianna sat up straight and looked down into the courtyard. Jonathan smiled up at her and waved.

"Yes, sweetheart," she said with forced good humor, "what is it?"

"Can I go for ice cream with Bruno and his mom?"

"Gelato," Bruno called, being helpful.

The boys grinned at each other. Jonathan was teaching his pal English; Bruno was reciprocating with lessons in Italian.

A happy arrangement, Bruno's mother called it. An unhappy arrangement, as far as Arianna was concerned. She knew it was foolish, but she didn't want her little boy turning into a Roman. He was American, not Italian. He wasn't Gianni, as even the *marchesa* now addressed him, he was Jonathan.

He wasn't Dominic's, he was hers.

"Mom? Can I go?"

"May I go," Arianna said automatically. She looked at the two boys and at Bruno's mother, Gina, who'd joined them and was smiling politely. The woman probably thought she was a terrible mother. "Yes. Yes, you may."

Jonathan and Bruno exchanged high fives.

"You could come, too, if you want."

Arianna knew the answer she should give; she could see the hopeful look on Jonathan's face, but even the thought of making the two block stroll while pretending to chatter happily with her pleasant neighbor made her stomach clench.

"I have a headache, sweetheart. I think I'll stay right here."

Gina clasped the children's hands. "It is the heat," she said politely. "It takes time to grow accustomed to it."

"Not for my mom," Jonathan said. "She grew up in Italy, right, Mommy?"

Worse and worse, Arianna thought, and answered the question with a question. "Would Bruno like to have supper with us tonight?"

Bruno bounced up and down with excitement. His mother laughed.

"I think that must be a 'yes.' "

"Good. Then I'll see you later."

Her neighbor waved, shooed the boys ahead of her through the gate that led from the cluster of elegant little houses and onto the *Via Giacomo*. Arianna watched the trio make their way along the narrow old street until they disappeared from view.

Then she sat back.

It would have been nice to go for ice cream with the boys and her new neighbor, who lived in the house next door. In fact, it would have been nice to become friends with her.

Jonathan and Bruno had discovered each other Jonathan's first day here, and Gina had gone out of her way to be welcoming, both to the little stranger from America and to Arianna.

Arianna sighed.

She'd been polite, but she hadn't been very gracious in return. *Thank you,* she said whenever Gina invited her for coffee, *but…*

After a while, Gina didn't bother asking. She said she understood.

"A newly married woman has much to do in her new home, *si?*"

She'd offered a woman-to-woman smile and Arianna had returned it, making them companionable conspirators in a world of happy brides and eager grooms.

What would her neighbor say if she knew the truth? That there were no happy brides or eager grooms in the Borghese household, that there were, instead, two people who maintained a polite front for the sake of a little boy…

That as far as Arianna was concerned, she had no new home.

She was imprisoned in a cage. Nobody could see the bars except her, but that didn't mean they weren't there. She was living in a city where she knew no one, with a man who'd all but bought her, and she had a secret so awful that it threatened to consume her.

She was depressed. Dominic was angry. Between them, they were miserable. That couldn't be anyone's definition of a marriage, not even his, though Arianna often wondered what, precisely, he'd thought he'd get for the purchase price he'd paid for her when he'd made his bargain back in the States.

A woman who loved him? Not that. Love hadn't been part of the deal. A woman who respected him? That hadn't been included, either.

Actually, she knew what he'd expected, that the passionate fuse they ignited would light again and make the arrangement acceptable, but she'd made it clear that she would not share his bed....

And he'd let her get away with it.

How come? Not that she'd change her mind, ever, but...but didn't it bother him, that he had a wife who wouldn't be his wife?

Arianna rose to her feet, picked up her empty glass and went into the house. The sitting room was dark and deliciously cool. She stood still for a moment, head lifted, eyes closed, and let the chill ease the pounding in her head.

He'd tried to make her play at being his wife in simpler ways, but she'd made her position clear on that, too.

"I have a housekeeper," he'd said the first morning, when he'd told her they'd eat breakfast together, for appearance's sake.

"I don't give a damn about appearances," Arianna had hissed, moments before Jonathan joined them, and Dominic had leaned toward her, his face dark.

"Do you give a damn about anything but yourself? Think of the boy. Use your head, Arianna. It will be better for him if he thinks we are happy together."

It was hard to argue with such logic and she hadn't even

tried. There were other ways to make Dominic understand how she felt about the arrangement he'd forced her into.

The simplest was to ignore his suggestion that she make whatever changes she wished in the apartment, and in how his housekeeper did things.

The woman had approached her that same morning.

"I was going to purchase new towels to replace the old in the first floor lavatory this week," Rosa had said politely. "Perhaps the *signora* would like to do it herself, or tell me what colors she prefers."

"Buy whatever you wish," Arianna had said, just as politely. "It doesn't matter to me."

"Well, then, if there are any special foods you like, *signora,* you have only to tell me and I'll be happy to prepare them."

"Thank you, but that's not necessary. Cook as you normally do."

A tiny frown had appeared in Rosa's forehead. "The boy has no favorites, either?"

Arianna had relented. Jonathan didn't like broccoli or cooked carrots. He loved chocolate milk. There was no reason not to tell all that to Rosa, especially since Jonathan's view of this change in their lives was the exact opposite of Arianna's.

Her son was thrilled. He loved Italy, loved Rome, loved the vast, high-ceilinged apartment with its marble and hardwood floors, its views of the *Via Giacomo,* the crowds that gathered on the Spanish Steps.

"I *love* it here," Jonathan had told her, holding his arms out wide to encompass all the new treasures of his young life.

What he loved most was Dominic—and the feeling was obviously mutual.

Dominic treated Jonathan in a way that would make most women ecstatic. Your new husband and your child were crazy about each other? Well, that was wonderful, wasn't it? Weren't the TV talk shows, the magazines, the pop psychology bestsellers everywhere full of sad stories of stepfathers who didn't like their new children? Of children who couldn't tolerate their stepfathers?

It wasn't like that in this family.

Man and boy chatted about anything and everything. Baseball. Soccer. Movies. Whether it was truly gross to suck up strands of pasta from your fork, or were there even grosser things nobody had yet invented. A new video game Bruno had talked about—a game that Dominic would surely bring home the next evening, despite Arianna's objections that he was spoiling Jonathan.

"He's a great kid," Dominic countered. "And I'm not spoiling him. I like to play these games, too."

He played with Jonathan after supper, while she read in the sitting room. Tried to read. It was hard, with the sounds of Dominic's laughter and Jonathan's giggles coming right through the door.

Last night, she'd watched them as they talked about baseball, something about a pitcher and the New York Yankees, and suddenly her heart had swelled with joy.

My son, she'd thought, my little boy and his father.

She must have made a sound because they'd both looked at her.

"Mom?" her son had said uncertainly, and she'd smiled and said, whoops, she was sorry, she'd just smothered a sneeze…and she'd gone to her bedroom, shut the door, leaned back against it and shuddered.

Her husband was a ruthless man. He'd proved that already, when he'd forced her into this marriage. What would he do if he figured out that Jonathan was his?

Arianna took a deep breath.

What was that old saying about putting the cart before the horse? There was no reason to think ahead. So far, nothing had changed. Dominic hadn't noticed anything. Maybe he never would. Women were good at speculation about who babies took after; men weren't. Hadn't she been part of endless conversations about the offspring of women she knew?

He has Jack's chin, one would say.

Natalie's eyes, another would add.

And the discussion would go on and on while the men in the group just rolled their eyes and finally, if pressed, one of them would crack that yeah, the kid in question looked like his old man but, basically, he just looked like a kid.

No, nothing had changed. Dominic would not catch on. He would remain a sperm donor who'd given her her son but didn't know it. He'd remain the husband she didn't want, didn't love, didn't desire...

Arianna swallowed hard.

She didn't. Of course, she didn't.

She walked slowly through the apartment, noting that Rosa had left things ready for dinner as she did each evening. The dining room table was set. Platters and covered dishes would be stacked in the refrigerator and on the big table near the stove.

God only knew what the housekeeper thought of the Borghese marriage. She arrived each morning at seven, just in time to see Dominic emerge from his bedroom and Arianna emerge from the guest suite with Jonathan. She'd looked startled, the first time she saw their strange morning entrances. Arianna knew enough about upper-class Italian marriages to know that separate bedrooms weren't unusual, but for newlyweds?

Surely, brides here shared their husbands' beds just as they did in the States.

The housekeeper probably thought the new *signora* was crazy. Well, maybe she was.

Arianna turned on the water in the kitchen sink and washed out her glass.

A woman would have to be crazy, wouldn't she, to get trapped in an arrangement like this?

Dominic made it seem as if he was a knight in shining armor, marrying her to keep the *marchesa* from collapsing that day in the back yard of the little house in Connecticut.

Who was he kidding?

Arianna put the glass in the drainer.

He'd made his incredible announcement, that he intended to force her into marriage, before the *marchesa's* arrival. He didn't like being reminded of that little fact, either. Apparently, he liked thinking of himself as a martyr who'd taken a wife as an act of gallantry.

The truth was that he'd taken a wife because he wanted one. Because he wanted her…and he hadn't done a thing about it. Not a thing.

All these nights, she'd slept alone. Slept? Not really. Mostly, she lay awake, despising Dominic, despising herself for not finding a way out of this nightmare…

…despising herself for wanting him.

Arianna sank into a chair at the kitchen table and buried her face in her hands.

The truth was ugly. She didn't want to face it, but denying it was even worse. She hated Dominic—and wanted him. Wanted him, night after night while she lay alone in her bed, staring up at the dark ceiling and remembering how it had been to make love with him, remembering the feel of his hands, the taste of his skin.

Last night, she'd been sure he was coming to her. She'd heard the creak of the floorboards and her heart had climbed into her throat. She'd sat up, clutched the blanket to her chin, waited, oh yes, waited for the door to open, for Dominic to step into the room, to come to her bed and take her in his arms, put an end to this nonsense and make her his wife.

But the footsteps had hesitated only briefly, then continued past her door the same as they did all the other nights.

And Arianna had awakened today as she did every day, detesting herself for wanting him.

The shame of it was a leaden weight lodged in her breast.

What kind of woman dreamed of possession by a man who'd forced her into marriage? Who would probably tear her son from her if he ever learned the truth?

Suddenly, the walls of the enormous apartment seemed to be pressing in. Arianna got to her feet and hurried to the front door. Maybe she could catch up to Gina and the boys. Maybe…

She fell back as the door swung open. Dominic stood on the threshold, eyes dark, mouth narrowed. He looked wild and dangerous, and her heart slammed into her throat.

"Arianna," he said, and what he wanted, what he intended, what he was, at last, going to do, all resonated in that one word.

Arianna turned and fled down the hall. She heard the door bang shut, heard the sound of her husband's footsteps coming after her. His hands clamped, hard, on her shoulders and he spun her toward him.

"No," she cried, and swung her fist. She caught him in the shoulder. Pain shot up her arm. Dominic's body, his muscles, everything about him was unyielding. She swung again. He grunted, dodged the blow, hoisted her into his arms and strode down the hall to the guest suite.

"Dominic!" She was panting, weeping as he elbowed open her bedroom door. "You can't. I won't—"

He bent his head, took her mouth with his. He bit her lip; she cried out in shock and when she did, he plunged his tongue inside. His taste, his heat, filled her. He slid his hand over her, cupped her breast, and she felt her nipple pearl under his rough touch.

Heat shot through her, quick and sharp.

"No," she said against his lips, but her body refused to go along with the lie. She moaned, arched against him. This. This, yes. This was what she wanted.

Dominic fell onto the bed still holding her, still kissing her. His heart thundered against hers as he slid his hand between them and began undoing the buttons on her blouse.

"Tell me," he growled. "Say it."

She couldn't. God, she couldn't, not even as she felt pleasure slipping along her skin like silk, even as she heard herself whispering his name.

Dominic cursed, gave up trying to open the buttons and tore the blouse open. Arianna lay exposed to him now. This was his, the lush curve of her breasts, the lightly perfumed cleft that dipped into a lacy white bra.

He kissed her mouth, kissed her throat, sucked at her nipples until she cried out in pleasure. She was clasping his shirt in her fists, writhing under him, against him, and he pushed up her skirt, slid his fingers inside her panties, watched her eyes blur with excitement.

She was hot. Wet. Ready. So ready. For him, only for him. The delicate scent of her arousal made him groan with desire.

"Say it," he urged, and she wound her hands around his biceps.

"Dominic," she whispered. "Dominic…"

Somewhere out on the hot Roman streets, a horn blared, then blared again. The commonplace sound jolted through Arianna, a sharp reminder of reality.

She froze, caught her breath.

What was she doing? Being taken in anger? Giving herself in anger? No. No…

"No!" The cry ripped from her throat.

She shoved against Dominic's shoulders. Pounded against them. He was blind, dumb, unaware of everything but his need. Sobbing, she hit him again. He caught her wrists and pinned her hands above her head.

"It's too late for that," he said roughly. "There's no turning back from what we both want."

"You forced me into marriage." Her voice trembled but

she kept her eyes on his. "Are you going to force me into sex, too?"

She felt his whole body tense. She waited, feeling the bite of his fingers into her flesh, afraid he might not stop—afraid of how she might respond if he didn't. Then, after a million years seemed to have gone by, Dominic spat out a word in the same dialect she'd heard him use before, let go of her wrists and rolled off her.

"To hell with this," he snarled. "To hell with you, and me, and this farce of a marriage."

He got to his feet and hurried from the room. Arianna scrambled up against the pillows, wincing as she heard his bedroom door bang shut. Then she rose from the bed...and saw her reflection in the mirror.

Her hair was a tangle of wild curls, her cheeks were flushed, her mouth swollen from Dominic's kisses. Her blouse hung in tatters; beneath it, her breasts showed patches of red from the scrape of stubble on his jaw.

Her teeth began to chatter. To think that he would do such a thing...

To think that she would let him.

That was the truth, wasn't it? That she'd let him ravish her. That she'd wanted him to do it, yearned for him to do it...

Footsteps sounded outside her door. She stumbled back, eyes wide, but the footsteps kept going. The front door slammed, and Arianna let out her breath.

Dominic was gone, at least for a little while.

She swung away from the mirror, pulled off what remained of her blouse and flung it into a corner. She snatched another blouse from the closet and put it on.

No more. She had to leave him, face whatever he'd do in retaliation. This couldn't continue, not even to protect the *marchesa,* not even to protect her dark secret about Jonathan...

She laughed, though it came out more like a sob. How

could she leave? Dominic held all the cards, and they both...

''Mah-mee. Hey, Mom.''

Oh God. Jonathan was back, shouting to her from the courtyard.

''Mom? Where are you?''

She shot to her feet, ran her hands through her hair, hurried through the apartment and onto the terrace.

Jonathan and Bruno grinned up at her, then waved madly as they slurped at cups of *gelato*. Bruno's mother was there, too, eating hers with a spoon.

For reasons Arianna would never quite understand, this moment would be frozen in her memory. In all the years to come, she'd remember it with complete clarity. Gina's smile, and the little boys with ice cream dripping down their chins, and the oppressiveness of the hot Roman afternoon...

And the sudden squeal of brakes, the horrendous shriek of tearing metal, the unending scream of a woman crying out in horror...

Mostly, she would remember knowing that something terrible had happened to her husband.

''Dominic?'' she whispered.

''Mommy?'' Jonathan said, his face gone white.

Gina's cup of ice cream fell to the ground.

''Come,'' she said, grabbing both boys, anchoring them to her sides and dragging them into her house.

Arianna flew into the apartment, through the endless expanse of rooms, down the stairs, out the front door, to the street...

And saw a woman, numb with shock, clutching a wailing infant in her arms.

Saw a charcoal-gray baby stroller lying overturned in the road, wheels spinning lazily.

Saw her husband's bright red car, its hood wrapped

around a lamp post, its front tires up on the curb, the driver's door flown open.

But what she saw that made her heart almost stop beating was Dominic, lying in the road beside the car, his arm bent at an angle that made her stomach roll, his head turned to the side, blood oozing slowly from his temple.

"Dominic," she whispered, but her voice rose to a scream as she ran to him, dropped to her knees, took his hand in hers and brought it to her lips.

Did his fingers offer the faintest pressure in return, or was it only her desperation that made it seem that way?

"Dominic," Arianna sobbed. She kissed his bruised knuckles and never left him until the paramedics came and gently but forcibly shifted her aside, so they could move her husband onto a gurney and put him in the ambulance.

CHAPTER NINE

WHY did people speak in whispers in hospitals?

Hospitals weren't quiet places like libraries. Hospitals were filled with noise. Bells rang with frightening urgency. Carts rattled as aides rolled them down the hall. Down at this end of the building, in the emergency section, there was a seemingly constant whirr of wheels as ambulance attendants rushed gurneys into the building, while doctors shouted instructions at nurses.

The only quiet thing in the entire place, as far as Arianna could tell, was her. She sat on a wooden bench outside Treatment Room One, hands tightly clasped, heart in her throat as she waited for word about Dominic.

Half an hour had passed since he'd been rushed into the white-tiled treatment room. A team of green-clad doctors and nurses had brushed Arianna aside, engulfed Dominic and lifted him onto an examining table.

"What happened here?" someone had barked, even as hands began undressing him.

"Motor vehicle accident," one of the EMTs said. "Victim swerved to avoid a baby carriage, climbed the curb and wrapped his car around a traffic barrier."

"Speeding?"

"No. Would have been a lot worse if he had."

"Seat belt?"

"No. He was thrown from the car. Probable compound fracture of the left humerus, possible concussion."

"Who's the orthopedist on duty? The neurosurgeon?"

"I'll find out," a nurse replied, and as she'd hurried to the door she'd noticed Arianna, pressed back against the wall. "You can't stay here," she'd said briskly. She'd put

123

a hand in the small of Arianna's back, pushed her into the hall, and drawn the curtains.

People had hurried in and out of the room ever since, but no one had paused to say anything to Arianna.

And she was going crazy, imagining what was happening beyond those curtains. What if Dominic didn't... What if he was seriously hurt? He'd been so white, so still. He might—he might—

Arianna shut her eyes. "Please," she whispered, "please, don't take him from me."

Dominic was alive. He had to be. He couldn't die. He couldn't leave her.

The curtains snapped back. Arianna shot to her feet as a woman in a hospital coat stepped briskly from the room, holding a clipboard and a pen.

"Signora Borghese?"

"Yes." Arianna tried to step past her but the woman obviously had experience with desperate family members and easily blocked her way. "How is my husband?"

"I must ask you some questions, *signora.* Is your husband allergic to any drugs?"

"I don't know. How is he?"

"Does he take any medications?"

"I don't know that either. Please, tell me—"

"Has he a history of heart disease? Diabetes? Stroke? Convulsions?"

Arianna stared at the woman. "Convulsions? Is he—oh God, please. Tell me what's happened."

The stern face softened, if only fractionally. "Nothing, *signora,* I promise. I'm simply trying to put together your husband's medical history. How about prior surgeries?"

Arianna shook her head.

"Hospitalizations? Broken bones? Concussions?"

"I don't know anything about his medical history! Please, is Dominic—how badly is he hurt?"

The woman capped her pen. "He has a break in the left

humerus.'' Arianna shook her head again and the woman touched the upper portion of her arm. ''Right here. It's a bad break, but there wasn't much tissue damage. Eight weeks, twelve at the most, in a cast and the arm will be fine.''

Something had been left unsaid. Arianna searched the woman's face.

''What else? I know there's more. My husband's head was bleeding. He was unconscious.''

''Yes. We believe he suffered a concussion. The doctor ordered a CAT scan. We'll know more once it's done.''

''But isn't he awake yet? Surely, by now…''

A look of compassion flashed in the other woman's eyes. ''No,'' she said gently, ''not yet.''

Arianna swayed unsteadily. The woman grasped her arm.

''You'll be no help to your husband if you fall apart, *signora*. Are you here alone? Shall I call someone to come and stay with you?''

Arianna shook her head again. There was no one to call. She had only an elderly grandmother and a small child. Dominic had never mentioned having a family and she had never asked. She'd never asked him anything about his life, she'd been too busy hating him, when all he was guilty of was wanting her—and wanting her son.

His son.

He'd tried to make the three of them into a family and she hadn't let him. Why hadn't she seen that until now?

''No,'' she said, ''there's no one. Thank you. I'll be—''

The curtains parted again. An attendant wheeled out a gurney on which Dominic lay motionless.

''Dominic,'' Arianna whispered, her voice breaking. She reached for his hand, clasped it tightly in hers and hurried alongside the gurney as the attendant wheeled it down a corridor, into an elevator, and then to a door marked Radiology, where they stopped her again.

''You'll have to wait outside, *signora*.''

Arianna leaned over Dominic and brushed her mouth gently against his.

"I'll be right here, *mio marito,*" she murmured.

The door swung shut.

She stared at it, drew a shuddering breath and turned blindly toward a bank of telephones on the wall.

She didn't know Gina's phone number but the operator found it for her and put the call through. Gina answered immediately, as if she'd been hovering near the phone and waiting for it to ring.

Gianni was fine; Arianna was not to worry about him. He'd had supper, he and Bruno were playing trains.

"And how is your husband?" Gina asked carefully.

"I don't know. It's too soon."

"I'll get Gianni."

Arianna closed her eyes and took a deep breath. She had to be strong when she spoke with her son.

"Mommy?" Her son's voice trembled.

"Yes, sweetheart."

"Did Dom'nic die?"

The childlike bluntness of the question shook her. "No," she said quickly, "no, baby. Dominic didn't die."

"What happened to him?"

She told him some of the truth. Yes, there'd been an accident. After that, she lied. Dominic was fine, the doctors said, but he'd have to stay in the hospital for a bit.

"Why?"

"Well, he broke his arm. Remember last year, when Billy Gooding broke his?"

"He had to wear a cast."

"Right, sweetheart. Dominic will have to wear one, too."

Jonathan's tone grew hopeful. "And we'll all write on it an' draw pictures?"

Arianna made a sound that was almost a laugh. "Yes. We'll all decorate his cast, baby. Okay?"

"Okay. Maybe I'll draw a picture of a cat." There was a brief pause. "How come Dom'nic has to stay in the hospital? Billy didn't."

"Well, Dominic hit his head, too. He'll have to stay here until the bump goes away."

"Oh." Another pause. "Mommy?"

"Yes?"

"Could you tell Dom'nic that I miss him?"

Tears welled in Arianna's eyes and streamed down her cheeks. "I'll tell him," she whispered.

Gina took the phone again, assured Arianna that she and her husband were happy to have Gianni spend the night, even the next few days. Arianna wiped her eyes, choked out a "thank you," ended the call and then, for the very first time, phoned Dominic's office.

He'd given her his private number. She'd countered by telling him it wasn't necessary.

"I can't imagine any circumstance under which I'd want to call you," she remembered saying.

Her throat constricted. How foolish she'd been. How selfish.

The phone rang and rang. Why wouldn't it? Nobody would answer a private number except Dominic, and he was here, locked away from her in a room filled with lights and machines...

"Dominic Borghese's office. This is the *signore's* assistant speaking. How may I help you?"

The voice was cool and professional, but it lost those qualities when Arianna identified herself as Dominic's wife.

"His wife? But the *signore* never mentioned..."

Arianna interrupted and explained what had happened.

"*Dio!* I felt in my bones that something was wrong. It is why I answered the telephone. *Signora,* my name is Celia. What can I do to help you?"

"I wondered," Arianna said, "I wondered if you would know...if you would know if my husband has a personal physician. They're doing everything they can here, but I want to be sure—to be sure—''

Her voice broke. She was going to weep again and tears didn't change anything. She'd learned that early, sobbing against the fates that had snatched her mother and father from her.

"I understand, *signora.* Yes, your husband has a doctor. I'll call him and have him meet you at the hospital, *si?*"

"Thank you. Tell him— Oh. They're bringing Dominic out."

"If you need anything else—"

"Yes. *Grazie.* I'll call you when I know more."

Arianna jammed the phone back on the wall. The attendant was wheeling Dominic's gurney down the corridor and she ran after it, but a hand closed on her arm.

"Signora Borghese? I'm the radiologist who took your husband's CAT scan. They're taking your husband to surgery, to set his arm."

Arianna tore her eyes from the gurney. "What did the CAT scan show? Is my husband—will he be all right?"

The radiologist nodded. The scan, he said, confirmed a concussion. With luck, there would be no swelling of the brain.

Without luck… Arianna couldn't bring herself to ask.

A tall, white-haired man hurried in and introduced himself as Dominic's personal physician. Arianna began asking questions. He held up a hand and stopped her.

"Give me a few minutes, *signora,* so I can speak with the doctors who examined your husband. Then we'll talk."

Arianna waited. And waited. Finally, the doctor returned. The arm would heal cleanly. The head… He touched her shoulder gently. The sooner Dominic regained consciousness, the better. Meanwhile, they'd moved him to a private room. If the *signora* would please wait just a little while…

But it was dark before a nurse finally told Arianna she could see her husband, and led her to a darkened room. It was the first truly quiet place she'd been in since coming to the hospital hours before.

Dominic lay still, as he had all afternoon. An IV was hooked to his arm; other tubes and lines snaked out from under the blanket.

Dominic, Arianna thought, *oh my husband.*

She took his hand and said his name. He didn't move, didn't so much as blink. Tears welled in her eyes. She leaned down and pressed her lips gently to his brow. Then she sat in a chair beside him, took his hand and waited.

She didn't really know what she was waiting for. A blip or a beep from one of the machines ranged alongside the bed? A word from a doctor?

She only knew that she would not leave this room until Dominic was with her again, until she could look into his eyes and tell him—and tell him—

Arianna's head fell back against the chair and she slept.

Hours passed. Then, just as the sun burnished the seven ancient hills of Rome with gold, Dominic began surfacing from unconsciousness to a sea of confused dreams.

He was alone in a vast room. Arianna was there, too, and he was hurrying toward her. He wanted to take his wife in his arms and tell her that she *was* his wife, by God, that he was tired of living like strangers, that he had married her because he wanted her in his bed.

In his life.

But no matter how many steps he took, he couldn't seem to close the distance between them. The room grew larger; Arianna's figure grew smaller. He called out her name and she spun away from him and began to run.

Dominic ran, too. Then he stopped. What was he doing, chasing after a woman who didn't want him?

A staircase yawned ahead. He ran down it to a shadowed street, jumped into his car, gunned the engine and started to drive away. He would leave Arianna, forget her…

He couldn't. Couldn't leave, couldn't forget. He put the car into a hard U-turn....

Il mio dio!

A woman pushing a stroller stepped out from between two parked cars. He swore, stood on the brakes. The woman jerked toward him, eyes widening with terror. Everything slowed, slowed—but not enough.

Dominic yanked the wheel to the right. The car, responsive as a thoroughbred, followed his command instantly. It spun, climbed the curb, shot ahead toward a concrete traffic barrier that blocked the *piazza,* and he knew he would never see his Arianna again.

Malleable metal struck unyielding concrete. Pain shot through his head, his body, and as a towering black wave of unconsciousness closed over him, he thought, with agonizing clarity, that it was too late. His pride had made him waste precious time. Arianna would never know—she would never know—

"Dominic?"

Dominic moaned and thrashed from side to side.

"Dominic," a soft voice pleaded urgently, "please, please open your eyes and come back to me."

Arianna's prayer was the strength he needed. Dominic opened his eyes and saw his wife leaning over him, smiling and crying at the same time.

"Arianna," he whispered, and when he did, she gave a sob and buried her face against his throat. He lifted the one arm that seemed to work, wrapped it around her and thought that he had never heard a woman weep as hard as his wife was weeping at this minute....

And that he had the world right here, in the curve of his arm.

"I have been in this prison a lifetime and I tell you all, I am not staying another day!"

Dominic sat up against the pillows, glaring at the little

group assembled at the foot of his bed. The orthopedist who'd tended his arm, the neurologist who'd consulted on the concussion, the charge nurse all stood with their arms folded and stern expressions on their faces.

His personal physician and his wife stood off to the side. His doctor looked amused; his wife looked—Dominic scowled. Who could tell? Women were good at wearing masks.

"You've only been here three days," the nurse said sternly. "That's hardly a lifetime, Signore Borghese."

"Have you ever been a patient in this place?"

"Well, no, but this is an excellent hospital, and—"

"And, it is a hospital. A place for sick people." Dominic sat up straighter. "Do I look sick to you?"

"But your arm," the orthopedist began.

"I broke it," Dominic said sharply. "You set it. Is there some magic mumbo-jumbo still to be performed that I don't know about?"

The orthopedist scratched his ear. "I guess not."

"Your turn," Dominic said to the neurologist. "Or don't you have a comment to make?"

"You had a concussion," the neurologist said mildly. "A bad one."

"I can walk and talk and perform all your ridiculous little tests. I've stood on one foot so long I began to think I was a stork, and I've touched my index finger to the tip of my nose enough times to be sure it's still there. Very scientific, that particular test." Dominic's jaw hardened. "Shall I repeat it for you with my thumb?"

The doctor grinned. "No, no, that's not necessary."

"Good. Then we are agreed. I am leaving this morning."

"But—"

"But, you have a choice. Sign me out, or I'll do it myself."

Dominic's physician sighed and stepped forward.

"Send him home, gentlemen. I've already discussed matters with Signora Borghese. Between the two of us, we'll keep an eye on him.''

Dominic looked at Arianna. He still couldn't read her expression. He hadn't been able to, not for the past three days. He still remembered waking at dawn the day after the accident, struggling up from a dream and finding his wife beside him, hearing her soft voice and then feeling the dampness of her tears against his throat as she wept in his embrace....

Unless that, too, had been a dream.

The nurse had come in, alerted by the machines he'd been hooked to, followed by the doctors, and Arianna had stepped back from the bed. The next time he saw her, hours later, he'd waited for her to tell him that she'd cried as he held her, that she'd pleaded with him to come back to her....

She hadn't said anything. And he hadn't asked. The neurologist had told him it was not unusual for a man waking from a coma to imagine things.

That was the probable answer.

It was too much to hope that Arianna would feel—that she would want—

Dominic cleared his throat. "Arianna?" He knew his expression gave nothing away. He watched his wife impassively, as he would in a boardroom when an important deal was on the table....

Or as he had watched his mother, years and years ago, when she'd told him she was moving to Milan and leaving him with a friend in Rome. He'd been twelve then, terrified but determined not to show it.

Dominic felt a muscle jump in his cheek.

He was thirty-four now, and suddenly he knew he was just as terrified.

All the more reason to show nothing.

"Arianna?" he said again. "Will it be a problem for you, having an invalid at home?"

Arianna bit her lip. She wanted to throw her arms around Dominic and tell him that she'd been praying for this day, that she wanted him home, home with her, more than she'd ever wanted anything in her life.

But Dominic was studying her as impersonally as he might have studied a stock report. It was the same way he'd looked at her for the past three days: politely, but with no real interest.

Those few moments when she'd wept in his embrace, when he'd held her close and whispered her name, might have happened a thousand years ago.

She'd been a fool to think it had meant anything, that the way he'd held her, the feel of his lips against her hair, was anything but the reaction of a man who'd cheated death.

"Arianna?" he said again. "Do you have any objection to having me at home?"

"No," she said politely, "none at all."

Dominic nodded. "Fine."

"Fine," she repeated, showing nothing, because even though her heart was filled with joy at the thought of having her husband back, she could see, very clearly, that he didn't feel the same way.

CHAPTER TEN

THEY went home in Dominic's limousine, the big car moving slowly through the early-morning streets.

Too slowly, evidently. Dominic leaned forward and spoke to the driver.

"I am not made of glass," he said impatiently. "Faster, yes?"

The man nodded and picked up the pace. Dominic settled into the corner again, glowering. Glowering was all he'd done since leaving the hospital, but Arianna wasn't surprised.

Her husband's activities were going to be restricted for a while. No going to work. No eye strain. No stress. Doctor's orders, all of it, and she'd been charged with the responsibility of seeing to it that Dominic obeyed.

She had about as much chance of that as a sand castle had of withstanding the tide. Dominic was not cut out to be a docile invalid. More to the point, all those restrictions meant he'd be trapped in the apartment with her.

The night he'd come out of the coma and held her close to his heart had less substance than a dream. Yes, he'd held her. But it hadn't meant anything. He'd been seeking comfort. She'd just happened to be there.

Still, she was his wife. She would be conscientious about his recovery. To that end, she'd done what she could to guarantee a quiet week.

Celia would phone twice a day to assure her boss that all was well. Dominic had wanted hourly calls but Arianna and Celia had closed ranks and agreed that twice a day check-ins would be more than sufficient.

Rosa would not come in at all. No vacuum cleaner running, no banging of pots and pans in the kitchen, no cheery voice singing operatic arias off-key. The apartment would be quiet.

Jonathan would be away, spending the week with the *marchesa.* This visit to Florence had been planned before the accident. Arianna smiled to herself. Her son was as thrilled with his new great-grandmother as she was with him. He'd been excited about the visit, but ready to cancel it after the accident.

"I want to see Dom'nic," he'd said.

Dominic had solved the problem by talking with his stepson on the phone.

"Do you really want to disappoint your *nonna?* She's been planning this visit for weeks. When you return from *Firenze,* we'll do a bunch of things together."

So Jonathan had agreed to stick to the schedule just as long as he could welcome his stepfather home this morning.

"I'm so glad Dom'nic's okay," he'd kept saying, with a look in his eyes that made it clear how much he worshipped him.

Arianna shot a quick look at Dominic. He was sitting as far from her as possible, staring straight ahead.

Her husband felt nothing for her, but he loved the son he didn't know was his. All those hours in the hospital that first day, waiting to learn if Dominic was going to be all right, she'd been haunted by the realization of how unforgivable it would be if father and son lost each other before learning the truth.

The lie she was living was wrong, but what could she do about it? She'd dug herself in so deep that there was no way out. Telling the truth was far, far too dangerous. Who knew how Dominic would react? What he would do? He was a powerful, vengeful man.

She might lose her child.

She was already losing her husband.

Once, knowing he'd married her for all the wrong reasons had filled her with anger. Now, he didn't want her at all. Not for whatever warped sense of revenge he'd thought she deserved, not for passion...not for anything.

That should have pleased her.

Why didn't it? What did she want from the man who was her husband? Hate? Love? Emotion of some kind. Any kind...

Not true. He'd shown her emotion the day of his accident and she'd rejected it. What if she hadn't stopped him? If she'd let herself be pulled down into that sea of passion.

Arianna's eyes blurred. She turned her face to the window as the car pulled up to the house. The chauffeur got out, but Dominic was already moving, reaching clumsily for the handle, muttering under his breath at the indignity of being helpless, when the door flew open.

"Dom'nic! Oh Dom'nic, you're home!"

Jonathan flung himself into Dominic's lap.

"Jonathan! Be careful. Dominic's arm—"

Arianna caught her bottom lip between her teeth. Man and child were embracing, her little boy laughing, her husband joining in, though his eyes were suspiciously damp.

"Hello, Gianni. Did you miss me?"

"Somethin' fierce!" Jonathan pulled back, his brow furrowed. "Mom told me you were all right, but I kept hearing the crash in my sleep, you know?"

Dominic nodded. "I know," he said gruffly.

"Even talking to you on the phone every day wasn't... I mean, sometimes I just thought, 'cause you were in a hospital and all..."

Dominic wrapped his good arm around the boy and drew him close. Arianna tried not to weep. Her child and his father loved each other so much.

What should she do?

Better still, what *could* she do, without bringing on disaster?

*   *   *

Jonathan left for the *marchesa's* an hour later and any pretense at polite conversation stopped.

Dominic went out on the main terrace, settled in a chaise longue and closed his eyes. Arianna stood beside him, waiting for him to acknowledge her presence. Was he going to ignore her for the entire week?

"Dominic? Shall I bring you something?"

"Nothing," he said politely. "Thank you."

"What about lunch? You must be hungry by—"

"Where is Rosa?"

"I gave her the week off."

Dominic opened his eyes. "You did what?"

"I gave her—"

"You should have consulted with me first."

"It's your home. She's your employee. I know that, but—"

"What *I* know is that I might need her assistance."

"For what?"

"How should I know for what? Making me lunch, for one thing. Finding me a shirt in the closet. I'm as helpless as an infant, in case you haven't noticed. How should I know what the hell I'll need her for until I do?"

"I'll be happy to help you," Arianna said calmly. "I've already made some sandwiches and some—"

"I don't need help from you."

The words snapped like a whip. Arianna stiffened under their lash, hating herself for the sudden tightness in her throat.

"Sorry. I forgot. You don't need anybody or anything. Not ever."

She whirled around, marched away from him and Dominic winced in expectation of a glass-rattling slam, but Arianna apparently controlled herself. The violent bang never came, though her body language had made it clear that was what she wanted to do.

Dominic sighed and laid his head back.

What was that all about? Had he even suggested he didn't need anybody or anything? No. He had not. Hadn't he just said he needed Rosa?

His wife was in a bad mood. That, at least, he understood. She hated him, hated Rome, hated the life he'd brought her to, and now she was trapped with him in this apartment for the next few weeks.

She probably figured the accident was all his fault, that he'd been angry and driving too fast, but that wasn't true. He'd just been coming back to take her in his arms and tell her he was sorry, that he hadn't meant to frighten her or hurt her, that he'd only wanted to make her see that—that—

What? That their marriage was a mistake?

Dominic closed his eyes. That's what it was, wasn't it? One hell of a mistake. How long could it go on? He couldn't share his space with Arianna much more, inhaling her scent, seeing her at breakfast and dinner and knowing she hated him, hated the existence he'd forced on her.

His head was pounding.

All right. This wasn't the time to make plans that stretched past tomorrow. He'd simply institute some changes so that she wasn't burdened with his care.

He'd call Rosa, tell her to resume her normal schedule even though the idea of pots rattling and the vacuum cleaner roaring made him shudder. And if Rosa launched into her ear-shattering rendition of Mimi in *La Bohème,* he'd have to threaten to murder her.

He'd call a temp agency, too, and hire a butler. A valet. *Dio,* just the idea of having someone wait on him made his belly churn, but he'd turned out to be damnably useless at simple things like buttoning his shirt or pulling on his trousers one-handed. He didn't even want to think about the intricacies of bathing.

Rosa couldn't help him with personal things like that and his wife surely couldn't. She wouldn't want to touch him.

To undo the buttons on his shirt, slip her hands under it so that he felt the cool press of her fingers against his skin...

Dominic groaned.

Wonderful. His arm was in a cast, his head was pounding, his wife despised him and he was turning himself on, just remembering what it had been like that first time, when she hadn't hated him, and imagining what it could be like again if the way she'd curled into his embrace that night in the hospital hadn't been a drug-induced dream.

If she felt what he did at the sight of her, this combination of need and desire and something more, something tender and gentle and—and—

"I'm sorry."

He looked up. Arianna stood over him, a tray in her hands, her expression as emotionless as the apology.

"No." Dominic sat up. "I'm the one who should apologize."

"It's all right. You're ill."

"I'm not ill. I have a broken arm. That's not an illness."

"You have a concussion. I shouldn't have yelled at you."

"I *had* a concussion. And you didn't yell."

"You're supposed to take it easy. And I did yell."

"No. You..." He paused and his lips turned up at the corners. "If we're not careful, we're going to end up fighting over who owes who an apology."

Arianna didn't answer. Then, slowly, she smiled.

"You're right. Okay, how's this? We were both wrong."

"That's perfect." Dominic looked at the tray and raised his eyebrows. "Are those tuna salad sandwiches?"

"Uh-huh." Arianna put the tray on the table beside him. "Rosa said you liked tuna."

"Did she shudder when she said it?" Dominic grinned as he reached for a sandwich. "She thinks anything made without garlic and proscuitto is fit only for *stranieri*."

"For foreigners. She told me."

"Ah. Then the good news is that she doesn't think of you as a foreigner."

"Don't be too sure. She said she could understand my liking tuna but the *signore,* after all, was Italian."

Dominic laughed. "She thinks I pick up bad habits when I visit the States."

"Yes. Well..." Arianna cleared her throat. "There's lemonade. Cookies, too. If you want anything else..."

She started to turn away. Dominic reached out and caught her wrist.

"Don't go."

"I don't want to bother you, Dominic. The doctor said—"

"Stay and have lunch with me. Please. It's my first day home. Keep me company."

He waited, his heart racing. How could it be so hard to wait for an answer to such a simple question?

"All right," she said slowly. "Thank you. I will."

It was, Arianna knew, a flag of peace. Dominic was envisioning the endless weeks ahead and making the best of the situation that he could.

Well, so could she.

They managed polite conversation during lunch and then during what remained of the afternoon. At seven, Arianna fled to the kitchen, grateful for the chance to make dinner.

She was exhausted from the strain of pretending she and Dominic were friends. Perhaps not even that. More like acquaintances. Surely not husband and wife. Not a man and woman who'd once come together in passion...

And created a child.

They ate in the dining room, Arianna at one end of the table, Dominic at the other. It was a beautiful room with white marble floors and pale, pale rose silk wallpaper. She'd thought about lighting candles and using them as a centerpiece, but dinner by candlelight was for lovers, not for them.

As at lunch, they made polite conversation. It didn't go as well as it had before. After a while, they fell silent. Dominic paid rapt attention to his plate, stabbing his fork into the pieces of meat Arianna had cut for him, poking at the potatoes and asparagus.

He didn't seem to eat much of anything.

"If you'd rather have something else…" Arianna finally said.

"What?" He looked up, his eyes met hers and then his gaze slid away. "Oh. No, this is fine."

"Is the meat too rare? I asked Rosa and she said—"

"It's fine."

"Rosa also said you like asparagus, but—"

"For God's sake, Arianna! Rosa isn't an expert on what I like and don't like. Why you would think…" He stopped, put down his fork and let out a long breath. "I'm sorry."

"No. No, that's all right. You must be—"

"Grumpy."

"Tired." Arianna pushed back her chair and stood up. "After all, your first day home…"

"Yes. Exactly." Dominic pushed back his chair, too. "I'll help you clean up."

"No!"

The word shot from her throat. The last thing she wanted was to spend more time with him and be reminded of how little he had to say to her, how uncomfortable he was just looking up and seeing her across the table. It was different when Jonathan was here. Alone—alone, she had to face the truth. She had no place in Dominic's life.

"I mean…" She forced a smile. "You should get some rest."

Rest? It was barely nine in the evening. Dominic suspected he would get no rest this night whatever the hour. He'd lie awake instead, seeing his wife's stiff smile as she pretended that spending almost an entire twelve hours alone with him wasn't a chore.

"Yes," he said quickly, "I think that's what I need. A good night's sleep." Was his smile as forced as hers? "That was an excellent meal. Thank you."

"I'm glad you enjoyed it."

"You're sure you don't mind if—"

"Of course not. Good night, Dominic."

"Good night." She turned away, then swung toward him. "Unless…?"

"Yes?"

Unless you want to have some coffee. Unless you don't want to leave me just yet. Unless you want to reach out, as I do, and bridge this chasm between us…

Arianna swallowed dryly. "Unless you, uh, you have objections, I thought I'd make a roast chicken tomorrow night."

A roast chicken. That was why she'd called him back. To discuss tomorrow's menu. Was that all they'd talk about in the endless days ahead? His taste in food and Rosa's knowledge of what he liked and didn't like? Maybe. What else could they discuss? What could Arianna say to him? Surely not the words he ached to hear, that she was happy he was home, that she was happy she'd married him, that— that—

"Roast chicken is fine," Dominic said, and fled to the safety of his bedroom.

Arianna stood staring after him. After a long moment, she began clearing the table. The day had been hot and muggy. Now, as darkness embraced the city, thunder rumbled far in the distance.

Wonderful. Just what this night needed. The drama of a thunderstorm, as if there wasn't enough drama hanging over this house already.

"Arianna?"

She turned and saw Dominic in the entry to the dining

room, his hair mussed, his shirt partly unbuttoned, and she knew with fearful clarity that the passion she'd felt for him the first time they'd met had never changed, would never change.

Thunder rolled through the sky again, an unwitting counterpoint to the sudden pounding of her blood.

"Yes?"

She saw his Adam's apple move up and down as he swallowed. "I'm—I'm sorry to bother you, Arianna, but—"

It was the first time she'd ever heard uncertainty in his voice.

"Are you in pain?" she said quickly. "I'll get the tablets the nurse—"

"I'm fine. It's just...I can't get these damn buttons undone."

Her eyes flew to the buttons that marched with military precision down the front of his pale blue shirt. Two were open. Two, just enough to form a vee that showed his tanned skin. The remaining buttons were still closed, all the way down to the black leather belt that circled his waist.

Arianna felt her face heat. Her eyes swept up and met his. He looked as miserable as a man could look. Well, why wouldn't he? He didn't like asking anyone for help, especially her.

"Oh. Of course. I should have offered..." She took a breath so deep she felt it all the way down to her toes. Then she smiled pleasantly and tried to ignore the way her hands had begun to tremble. "I'll get them for you."

He stood unmoving as she came to him, his eyes locked to her face.

"I sprained my wrist a couple of years ago," she said, reaching for the first closed button. "I couldn't believe how useless it made me feel."

One button undone. Why didn't he say anything?

"It was my left wrist and I'm right-handed, like you, so I thought, well, this isn't going to be a problem."

Two buttons. More of his chest was visible. Tanned skin, muscled pectorals, dark whorls of hair. Wasn't he going to say anything? Was he just going to let her chatter like an idiot?

"But it was. A problem, I mean. I had an awful time with the silliest things. Like—like putting up my hair. It was longer then, and—"

"You have beautiful hair, Arianna."

Her fingers stilled on the button. His voice was so low. So rough. The sound of it sent a tremor of electricity dancing down her spine.

"Thank you. That won't be a problem for you, at least. I mean, your hair is short. Not that I won't help with it, if you ask. Wash it. Comb it. Or…" She clamped her lips together. *Stop babbling!* "There! Just one last—"

"Take it down."

Her eyes flew to his. "What?"

"Your hair. Take it down."

"Dominic." Arianna swallowed hard. "I don't think—"

"Please. Take out those clips and let your hair loose."

She didn't have to make the decision. He'd made it for them both. His hand was in her hair; the clips at her temples dropped to the floor and he combed his fingers through the pale strands.

"I never forgot the feel of your hair against my mouth, Arianna. Against my skin."

"Dominic." God, she could hardly breathe. The way he was stroking her cheek, his hand warm against her face… She looked up. "Dominic," she whispered, "what—what are you…"

He kissed her. Gently, tenderly, the brush of his lips like silk, as soft as the whisper of his fingers against her cheek. She stood trembling, breath stilled, and then she made an almost imperceptible sound and he kissed her again, his mouth searing hers with its heat, holding her only that way, with a kiss, until she felt as if she would melt.

Lightning sizzled outside the window.

A moment later, a lifetime later, Dominic lifted his head. Arianna swayed unsteadily. Her eyes met his as he cupped her jaw, slid his thumb over her bottom lip.

"Say it," he whispered. "Arianna. Tell me what you want."

I want you to love me.

The truth, so long concealed within her heart, was stunning and as dangerous as the lightning bolt that slashed the black sky. She knew he waited to hear her say that she wanted to make love with him...but now she knew that would never be enough.

She loved Dominic.

And what was worse, she wanted him to love her.

How many secrets could a woman live with before she broke?

Something must have shown in her face. Dominic dropped his hand to his side and took a step back.

"It's all right." His voice was thick; she could tell what letting go of her had cost him. "I shouldn't have asked." She shook her head, put her hand on his arm and he stepped away again, as if her touch burned him. "Really, it's all right, *cara.* It's been a very long day."

"Dominic, wait..."

He walked away and she stood in the center of the room, feeling numb as she watched him go.

She heard his door shut. The storm, growing nearer, sent a gust of wind howling through the trees in the courtyard.

Arianna wanted to howl, too. Howl, and weep, and beat her fists against the wall, but she wouldn't. Feeling sorry for herself had never helped, not when her parents died, not when she'd learned she was pregnant. What had gotten her through, each time, was facing the truth.

That was what she had to do now.

She had to find a way to end this sham of a marriage, fall out of love with a man who didn't love her, and tell him he had a son. Nothing to it, she thought, and gave a choked, painful laugh.

She slept fitfully, tumbling in and out of an endless dream in which she walked a long, narrow path beneath a sky where thunder rolled endlessly and lightning lit the somber clouds.

She was alone. So terribly alone.

A roll of real thunder from the storm outside the house rattled the windows. Arianna shot up in bed, shaking from the dream.

Lightning lit the room. There was a distant hiss, as if a giant cat were showing its displeasure, and the illuminated face of the bedside clock went dark. So did the world. Not even a glimmer of light shone through the windows from the street.

Her heart thudded. She'd been terrified of storms like this when she was little. Her parents had understood. Her grandmother hadn't.

"Don't be a coward, Arianna," the *marchesa* would say when she found her hiding in a corner as a storm pounded the sky above the *palazzo*. "Del Vecchios are never afraid."

She'd stopped being afraid. Of life, of loss, of violent storms, but tonight she might as well have been a little girl again, frightened of the roar of thunder, of the jagged streaks of lightning, of the thick, black darkness...

Of the emptiness in her heart.

"Dominic," she whispered brokenly, "oh Dominic."

The door swung open. A bright beam of light pierced the darkness, found her huddled against the pillows. Arianna threw up a hand against the glare—against the risk of letting Dominic see her tear-streaked face.

"Arianna?" He swung the flashlight away from her. "Are you all right?"

"Fine," she said brightly.

"It's a bad storm. I thought it might have awakened you, and then when the lights went out…"

"Really. I'm—" another roar of thunder "—fine."

Dominic didn't believe it. She didn't sound as if she were fine. She sounded terrified.

"Arianna," he said gently, "it's all right to admit you're afraid."

"I'm not."

"*Cara,* everyone is afraid of something. It's not a sign of weakness to admit it."

"I'm not a child, Dominic. I know that."

"All right. In that case, I'll leave you the flashlight. If you need me—"

"I won't. I keep telling you, I'm—"

Thunder roared directly overhead. Lightning slashed through the darkness, and Arianna almost jumped from the bed.

The hell with this, Dominic thought. She was frightened, she was his wife, and it didn't matter that she'd been making it clear for more than a month that she didn't need him. He wouldn't be much of a man if he turned his back and walked away.

He was beside her a second later, curving his one good arm around her, drawing her close against his naked chest.

"I'll take care of you, *cara,*" he whispered. "Just lean against me."

It was the second time he'd offered her his strength, but she didn't need it. Didn't need anything. Didn't need him…

He slid his fingers into her hair and slowly raised her face to his. For one endless moment, Arianna held back. Dominic whispered her name again, his voice so tender, so filled with need, that she felt her fear give way.

"Dominic," she whispered.

She clasped the back of her husband's head, drew his face down to hers and kissed him.

CHAPTER ELEVEN

DOMINIC groaned as their lips met.

The years spent without Arianna faded away. All that mattered was the taste, the touch, the sweet pleasure of holding her close again.

He'd tried to put memories of a nameless woman and the one night they'd shared behind him but he'd never managed to do it. Now, he'd found her and made her his wife.

And this—this was their wedding night.

His kisses deepened. Was he moving too fast, asking too much? No. He wasn't. Arianna was returning kiss for kiss; she was touching him, moving her cool hands over his face, his shoulders, his chest. He murmured her name, cupped her breast through her thin nightgown and she shuddered with pleasure.

"Dominic," she sighed, and his body tightened like a fist.

He told himself to slow down. This wasn't a hurried coupling of strangers. This was Arianna, his wife, holding him as if she never wanted to let him go.

He could linger over the flicker of her tongue against his. The little moans humming in her throat. The way she arched toward him as he bit lightly at her nipples through the cotton gown. There was time for all that and more. He could take her to the edge of eternity and keep her there until she was wild for his possession.

But she was wild already, writhing in his arms, sobbing his name, and he was on fire, so hard and swollen that his erection throbbed against her belly.

Still, he needed her to tell him she wanted him, longed

for him, that she'd spent the last years remembering, just as he had.

She was saying it with every kiss. Why wasn't it enough?

"Dominic."

Had his name ever sounded so sweet on a woman's lips? Soft. Tender. As if she spoke it from her heart. The storm had stopped; a quarter moon had risen and in its watery light he looked at Arianna's face and saw something in her eyes, something that filled him with joy.

"Arianna. *Come sei bella.*" He drew her closer, kissed her, fell back on the bed with her and a sharp pain lanced through his arm. The breath hissed between his teeth and Arianna reared back.

"What? Oh. Oh, your arm! Dominic, I should have thought—"

Pain still shimmered through him but he caught her wrist, brought her hand to his mouth.

"Don't pull away."

"But your arm..."

"I'm all right."

"You aren't. I don't want to hurt you."

He pressed a kiss into her palm, nipped gently at the soft flesh at the base of her thumb.

"You could only hurt me by leaving me now."

It was true. The pain was subsiding. All he needed was the soft feel of his wife as she sank down against him.

He tangled his fingers in her hair and brought her mouth to his for a slow, deep kiss. *Dio,* the sweetness of her mouth. The way she sighed as their lips met, so that the soft whisper of sound became part of the kiss.

"Arianna." His voice was husky with need. "I want to see you, but I can't undress you, not with one hand. Do it for me. Take off your gown, *mia principessa.*"

She wanted to, wanted his hands on her skin. It was five years since she'd been with a man. There'd been no one since Dominic.

Now, he was her lover again.

And he was her husband.

The realization excited her. To bare herself to her husband. To have, at last, the wedding night she had denied them both.

"Undress for me, Arianna."

Nerves warred with anticipation. Her body had changed since he'd last seen it. She was rounder. Fuller. Would he notice? Would he find her beautiful still?

"Cara." He ran his hand down her back, stroking, caressing. "Let me see you."

Arianna slicked the tip of her tongue over her lips. Then she got to her knees beside him and slowly drew her nightgown over her head.

Moonlight scattered wisps of ivory light over her skin.

Dominic looked at her, his eyes moving slowly from her face to her breasts to the gentle curve of her belly.

"I—I've changed," she said unsteadily.

She had. Time and the birth of a child had turned her from a beautiful girl to an exquisite woman. For a heartbeat, he felt a pain that had nothing to do with his broken arm. If only he were the man who'd given her that child…

Arianna crossed her arms over her breasts. "Maybe this—maybe this wasn't such a good idea."

Dominic smiled. "It's the best idea I've ever had," he said gently. He kissed the curves of her breasts. "You're more beautiful than before, *cara,* so beautiful you take my breath away." Eyes locked to hers, he eased her arms to her sides. "My only wish is that we hadn't spent all these years apart."

Tears rose in Arianna's eyes. "Mine, too."

He reached out, touched the tip of his finger lightly to the dusty rose center of one breast.

"But we're together again. That's all that matters."

He moved his thumb, his hand, and she moaned.

"You have beautiful breasts, *cara.*" His hand drifted

down the valley between them, glided over her stomach, cupped the feminine delta between her thighs.

"And this part of you, this place I remember because it is where the taste of you was the sweetest..."

"Dominic." Arianna caught his hand. "If you do that—if you do that—"

"What?" His voice became thick. "What will happen if I do that, Arianna?"

She closed her eyes as he slipped his hand between her thighs and found her. It was too much. It was too much...

And it wasn't enough. She needed more. Needed—

"Please," she whispered, "please."

"Tell me."

"Make love to me. Come inside me. Oh God, Dominic, I need you, need you—"

Her cries made his blood pound. Between them, they tugged off his sweatpants. His erection sprang free. Arianna caught her breath, touched him, felt the velvet-encased hardness of him pulse against her hand, and instinct took over.

"Dominic," she whispered, "my husband."

Eyes on his face, she lowered herself on him, took him slowly inside her, deep inside her, her cry of pleasure a sweet counterpoint to his husky groan of satisfaction.

This, oh this was everything. Dominic, filling her. Dominic, his eyes dark with passion. Dominic, his hand curved around her hip, his breathing quickening as she began to move.

His touch, his whispers, urged her on. Her head fell back; she rode him hard, no inhibitions, no shame. Love had driven her past those barriers to a place she'd never believed existed.

Dominic watched his wife moving above him. Her body glistened with sweat; her hair fell in a tumble down her back. She was the most beautiful woman who had ever lived and she was his.

He groaned, felt the tightening in his groin, but he forced himself to hold back. He wanted to watch his Arianna as she flew toward the stars. When she cried out his name and convulsed around him, he pulled her down to him, rolled above her and let go of everything, his heart, his soul, his dreams, everything he was or ever would be.

He felt her come again as the power of his orgasm shuddered through him. Their cries of release mingled and when he bent his head, kissed Arianna and tasted the salt of tears, he didn't know if they were hers or his.

"Dominic." His wife's voice broke. "Dominic, *nonlo lasci mai.*"

"I won't," he whispered, "I'll never leave you, *cara mia.* Never."

Still joined, he stirred inside her, kissed her, and as they began the journey to the stars again, Dominic finally faced the truth.

He'd married Arianna for only one reason.

He loved her.

Time passed. Moments, hours—what did it matter?

Arianna sighed and stroked her hand lightly down Dominic's back. His skin was warm and supple, the muscles beneath it hard and well-defined.

"Are you all right, sweetheart?" he murmured.

She smiled. "I am very all right."

Dominic smiled, too. He rolled to his side, still holding Arianna against him. "Yes. You most certainly are," he said, brushing his mouth softly over hers. "It was enough, then? The way we made love?"

"It was wonderful." A blush colored her cheeks. "Was it all right for you? Having me on top?"

"Well," he said thoughtfully, "I'm not sure."

"Oh. I thought—I mean, I never—"

"Arianna." Dominic caught a handful of her hair and gently tugged her face up to his. "I'm teasing you, *cara.*

It was incredible. I was just hoping to convince you we'd have to try it a couple of dozen more times. Strictly so I could give you an opinion, of course.''

"Ah. Well, I suppose, in that case…''

Her lips curved in a smile. He smiled, too, and then he kissed her, lay back and drew her head to his chest. "I was a fool, five years ago, Arianna.''

"No. It was me. I should never have sneaked off but it all seemed so—so wrong. What we did. What *I* did. I'd never—''

"Neither had I, *cara,* but then, I'd never wanted a woman as I wanted you…as I want you still.''

Another kiss, longer and deeper than the last. Dominic sighed. "I thought about hiring someone to find you.'' He stroked his hand over her hair, toying with the soft curls that wound lightly around his fingers. "Then I thought, but if she didn't care enough to leave me her name…''

"I was embarrassed.''

"*Si.* I know that now, but then…'' He sighed again. "A man can make a fool of himself, *cara,* trying to protect his precious pride. I convinced myself it was best to forget you.'' His voice roughened. "But I never did.''

"I never forgot you, either,'' Arianna admitted softly. "I dreamed about you, fantasized about walking into a room and finding you waiting for me.''

Dominic drew her closer. "I'm here now, *cara,* and we'll never lose each other again.''

There was a sudden tightness in Arianna's throat. She loved this man so much! How could she have lied to herself for so long?

And how could she go on lying to him?

Honesty was important in any relationship but especially in this one. Dominic had made that clear. He'd taken her as his wife because he hadn't wanted a marriage built on lies.

And theirs was built on the worst possible kind of lie. He had a son, and he had the right to know it.

Now, Arianna thought. Right now, before her courage failed.

But Dominic was whispering to her, caressing her...

And she was lost to everything but his touch.

He said he would make breakfast, if she would tell him how to do it.

Arianna gave a dramatic sigh, told him to sit at the kitchen counter and drink his orange juice and she would make breakfast for them both.

He sat down and watched his wife bustle back and forth. It was a wonderful sight, he thought, and grinned.

Arianna caught the grin out of the corner of her eye.

"What?"

"Nothing."

"Nothing, the man says." She turned the bacon in the skillet, then reached for the eggs. "I saw that smirk, *signore.* You can't tell me it was nothing."

Dominic raised his glass to his lips. "I was just thinking that you're a definite improvement over Rosa."

She laughed. "Wait until you taste your bacon. You might not agree."

"No, I don't think I'll change my mind, not even if you burn the bacon." He cupped his chin in his hand, rested his elbow on the countertop and regarded her thoughtfully. "For one thing, you're easier on the eyes."

Rosa probably weighed 250 pounds. Arianna tried not to smile.

"That's nice to hear."

"And you don't harbor a burning desire to sing at La Scala."

"You haven't heard me in the shower, or you wouldn't even joke about the possibility."

Dominic raised his eyebrows. "You didn't sing a note

when we shared the tub a little while ago.'' A smile tugged at the corner of his mouth. ''Of course, I suppose, even one-armed, I did a pretty good job of keeping your mind off everything, but—''

Arianna leaned over the counter and silenced him with a kiss.

''Stop boasting,'' she said softly, ''and tell me how you like your eggs.''

''Cooked.''

''Oh, you're funny today, *signore*.''

''I'm happy,'' he said simply. ''Aren't you, *signora?*''

She looked at him. ''Yes. Oh yes, I am.''

They smiled at each other and then Arianna sighed and reached for the eggs.

''The bacon really will burn if I don't make the eggs soon. How do you want them?''

''Scrambled, wife.''

He said the word teasingly but it sent a tremor of pleasure through her. She looked at him, her lips curving in a smile. He smiled back. She cleared her throat. If she didn't make those eggs soon, they'd both forget all about breakfast.

And they couldn't do that because after breakfast, if she didn't lose her courage completely…

''Scrambled,'' he said, ''with cream, not milk.''

''Cream's bad for you.''

''Maybe. But it makes the eggs cook up softer,'' he said with the authority of a man who'd washed dishes in a Roman *trattoria* for three months when he was seventeen.

''It makes your arteries scream with terror.''

He grinned. ''I'm too young to have talking arteries.''

Arianna leaned over and kissed him again. He cupped the back of her head and deepened the kiss. After a moment, she sighed and drew back.

''I think I'd better make those eggs,'' she whispered. She

touched her finger to his mouth. "To keep up your strength."

They smiled at each other. She turned away and he watched her whip the eggs. Well, not really. What he was really watching was the way her delectable bottom wiggled from side to side.

She was wearing a T-shirt and panties. He'd wanted her naked; she'd looked at him as if he'd lost his sanity so they'd compromised. Jeans for him, the panties and T-shirt for her.

And what a fine compromise it was.

Dio, he was a lucky man. A beautiful wife who loved him, for surely she did, even if she hadn't yet said the words. And a child he adored almost as if the boy were his own.

Untrue. He loved the boy *exactly* as if he were his own. What if he adopted Gianni? That would make them father and son. A real family.

The thought filled him with happiness. He rose from the stool, grabbed two plates and brought them to the stove just as Arianna turned off the burner.

"Let's eat on the terrace."

She blinked. "I can't go outside like this!"

"The terrace off my bedroom is private. Nobody can see us."

"Dominic…"

"Outside," he said firmly, and scooped the eggs and bacon onto the plates.

Arianna rolled her eyes, grabbed napkins and silverware and followed him.

He was right. The terrace was heavily screened with pots of tall flowering plants. Arianna sank into a chair, felt the warm kiss of the sun on her face and the soft pressure of her husband's mouth on the nape of her neck and wondered if any woman had ever been as happy as she was today.

Without warning, a coldness stole into her bones. She'd

never been superstitious, but the *marchesa* had once employed a housekeeper who'd believed in evil eyes and all the rest.

Never let the gods know you're happy, the woman would mutter darkly, *or they'll go out of their way to make you suffer.*

Arianna shuddered.

"What is it, *cara?* Are you cool? We'll go back inside."

"No," she said quickly, "I'm fine. I'm just—I'm just so…"

Dominic leaned closer. "Happy," he whispered.

She nodded, so filled with emotion she was afraid to speak.

"*Si.* I understand. It's almost too much. For me, too."

Their eyes met. The expression on Dominic's face made her breathing quicken.

"Breakfast can wait," he said gruffly, and he drew her down onto a chaise longue hidden like a secret island within a bower of flowers and made love to her until she could think of nothing but him.

This time, when Dominic asked if she wanted to see his Rome, Arianna said yes.

He phoned for his driver who took them to the Forum, to the Capitoline Hill, to the Coliseum and to all the places she'd visited a hundred times as a child but never really seen until now.

Then he said he wanted to show her something outside the city.

"I wish my arm weren't in this damned cast and sling. We could go by ourselves, without a chauffeur."

"I can drive."

"But my car is a Ferrari. A brand-new one."

She knew it was. The dealership had delivered the car to the house the day after Dominic's return from the hospital.

"How nice," she said politely, pretending she didn't

hear the unease in his voice. "And how convenient, that I can drive a stick shift."

She almost laughed at the look on his face, but he surprised her.

"Well," he said, and cleared his throat, "that's fine. We'll go back to the apartment, get the car and take a drive. There's something I want you to see."

Tension radiated from his body in almost palpable waves for the first twenty minutes of the journey. Arianna bit her lip as he offered helpful advice.

That's a turn up ahead.

Must you really pass that car?

And her favorite, delivered with admirable wariness: *Maybe you're driving too fast,* cara, *what do you think?*

What she thought was that she'd yet to go above fifty and she knew, from things Celia had said, that Dominic probably never drove below that speed, especially on a road like this. But she held her tongue and after a while, when she saw him begin to relax, she glanced at him and smiled.

"It's a lovely car, Dominic."

"And you drive it well."

"Thank you. I love to drive. I only learned how a few years ago." She shot him another smile. "The *marchesa* thought women who drove were, you know, kind of fast.'"

He laughed. "I'm not surprised." They drove in silence for another few minutes. "Did you learn to drive after you bought the house in Connecticut?"

"Before that. I liked the idea of getting out of the city for an occasional weekend."

"Ah. I thought perhaps, after you had Gianni— Jonathan—"

"Gianni." Arianna moistened her lips. "It's a good name, perfect for—for my son. I'm sorry I was so stupid about using it."

"You weren't stupid, *cara*," Dominic said softly. "He

is, as you said, your son. I was wrong to insist on using something other than his given name.''

''Well, let's agree that we were both wrong and that, from now on, his name is Gianni.''

Dominic smiled. ''Good.'' He waited a minute. ''The man who is his father... You said he doesn't know.''

Arianna felt as if a hand had reached into her chest and wrapped around her heart.

''That's right.''

''You didn't think he'd want to know he had a child, you said.''

''Uh huh.''

''Because, God knows, if I had a son—''

''When I made it, it was the right decision.''

''I'm sure. I'm not second-guessing, *cara,* I'm just trying to imagine what it must have been like for you, finding yourself pregnant and having nobody to turn to.''

Her hands tightened on the steering wheel. ''It was like everything else in life,'' she said lightly. ''Things happen, you live through them. Besides, it was an easy pregnancy. I was fine.''

''For which I shall be eternally grateful,'' he said, and smiled. ''As for Gianni—you're done a wonderful job of raising him.''

''Thank you.''

''He is a son any man would be proud of.''

''Thank you again.'' *Where was this conversation heading?* She wanted to tell him about Gianni, but not while they raced along a road in the middle of nowhere.

''That's what I want to talk to you about, Arianna... Oh. Do you see that turn ahead? Take it, please.''

She made the turn onto a road even more dusty and narrow than the one they'd been driving. Tall pines rose up on either side, filtering the sun and offering welcome relief from the heat.

''Where are we going?''

"Another minute or two... There. Up ahead. See it?"

What she saw was a white villa, rising as if in a dream against a backdrop of dark green hills. She slowed the car as they entered a circular driveway, drove past a white marble Diana, her hunting dogs at her heels, pouring water from a brass ewer into a travertine marble fountain.

"Pull over," Dominic said, his voice a little rough.

"Are we visiting someone?" Arianna put her hand to her hair. "If I'd known..."

"No one lives here. No one has, for a long time."

Dominic stepped from the car, came around to the driver's side and pulled open the door. His cheeks were strangely flushed. For a moment, she worried that he might have a fever, but when she gave him her hand his fingers were icy cold.

"I first saw this house many years ago," he said softly.

He led her up the wide marble steps to the front door. He pulled a key from his pocket, opened the door and motioned her ahead of him.

Arianna gasped with delight. The house was unfurnished but it was easy to see its timeless beauty.

"Oh, Dominic, it's beautiful."

"I think so, too." Pride edged his voice. "I helped restore it."

She swung toward him. "You?"

"I wasn't always a rich man, *cara*. Surely you've heard the stories about me. About my background."

"I never listen to gossip," she said softly, "and whatever I did hear doesn't matter."

"Still, you have the right to know the truth about the man you married." Dominic drew her forward, walking slowly through the graceful, empty rooms. "I was born a bastard," he said simply, "and grew up on the streets of Rome. I have no idea who sired me, and my mother walked out of my life when I was still a kid."

"Dominic." She turned toward him and put her hands on his shoulders. "It doesn't matter."

"But it does." He clasped one of her hands and brought it to his lips. "You see, I'm not foolish, *cara*. All the jokes people make about men not being in touch with their feelings…" He smiled. "It's not true. We're in touch. We just choose to ignore them." His smile faded. "I know, for instance, that the reason I never wanted to trust a woman with my heart was because my mother broke it."

Arianna's throat constricted. "Please. You don't—"

"Let me finish, *cara*. It wasn't easy, working up to this, but I owe it to you."

"You don't owe me any—"

He bent to her, kissed her mouth gently, then put his arm around her shoulders. They began walking again, down airy corridors, through silent rooms.

"As a boy, I did things I'm not proud of. I lied to tourists, I picked pockets, I did whatever I had to do to survive and I told myself it was nothing even close to what the world owed me. Then, one day, I got caught with my hand in a tourist's pocket. I was arrested, jailed… I was out in thirty days, but I vowed I'd never lose my freedom again. So I looked for work. One place I found it was here, as a laborer." His mouth twisted. "I laid bricks, pounded nails, and learned for the second time that it was foolish to trust my heart to a woman. It was the final lesson, *cara*. I knew I wouldn't make the same mistake again. So I went out into the world, worked my way across Italy doing construction, landed in Sicily, and ended up working for a man most of Italy feared."

"Dominic. Please. You don't have to—"

"Arianna." He laughed, cupped her chin and kissed her. "Are you afraid I'm going to tell you I'm part of some dangerous *famiglia?* No, sweetheart, I'm not. The work I did was very simple. I helped him build a house. This man had a good heart, even if he kept it well hidden. He liked me. I liked him. He came to treat me almost as a son. And when he died two years later—peacefully," he said, with a quick smile, "he left me a legacy."

"And that was the start of Borghese International?"

Dominic shook his head. "It was a very small legacy, *cara*, though it was a lot to me back then. I was amazed and grateful, and used the money as a stepping stone." He drew her closer. "I'd heard about emeralds in the jungles of Brazil...and I got lucky. Eventually, I was no longer Dominic Borghese, construction worker. I was Borghese International. I had wealth, power, everything...but I didn't have the only thing a man really needs." He paused, and his voice softened. "I didn't have a family. Now, thanks to you, I do."

Tears had risen in Arianna's eyes. "Dominic. My darling Dominic. I'm so sorry. So very sorry you lived such a hard life."

"Don't be. I didn't tell you this story to make you weep but to make you see what you—and Gianni—mean to me." Dominic cleared his throat. "And to see, too, why it was so hard for me to trust you. To let you inside here," he said, tapping his heart, "where I vowed never to be hurt again." Dominic took an unsteady breath. "I want us to marry again, *cara*. A real wedding this time, you in a white gown, me in one of those silly suits men wear on such days."

He paused, drew himself together. "And if you will permit it, I want to do one other thing to make us a real family. I want to adopt Gianni and make him truly my son."

A sob burst from Arianna's throat. Dominic felt his heart turn heavy. She didn't want these things. It was her right, he knew that, but—

"Dominic." She put out her hand, touched his face. "All the things you said about trust. About never letting anyone hurt you again..." Her voice cracked. "I love you," she whispered. "Think of that, remember it, believe in it."

Those were the words he'd waited to hear. Then, why was a coldness wrapping around him?

"What are you trying to tell me, Arianna?"

She took a steadying breath. "I lied to you about Gianni's father. He isn't someone in the past."

His face went blank. "What does that mean?"

"It means there's no need for you to adopt Gianni because—because Gianni is your son."

CHAPTER TWELVE

DOMINIC rocked back on his heels. Arianna remembered when he'd fought with Jeff Gooding, how none of Jeff's blows had hurt him.

What she'd just told him made him reel.

"Dominic, please..."

He stepped back from the hand she held out. "Am I supposed to believe this? That Gianni is my son?"

"It's true. He's yours. That night we made love..."

"One night, Arianna. That was all. Just one night."

"That was enough. I got pregnant."

"You got pregnant." His voice was as flat as his eyes. "I used condoms."

"I know. I don't know what happened. An accident..."

A muscle began to tic in his jaw. "How are you so certain the boy is mine?"

She didn't flinch. It was a brutal question, but she supposed she deserved it.

"Because I wasn't with anyone else. Not for months before. And not after. You were the only one. I didn't sleep with anybody else."

"There are tests," he said coldly.

"Do them. They'll all prove the same thing. You're Gianni's—Jonathan's—father."

Dominic stared at her. "I thought," he said slowly, "when I first saw him, I thought..."

"Yes. I was afraid you would."

"His coloring. His eyes. The way he smiles..." He thrust his hand into his hair, swung away from her and paced across the room. "Mine. The boy is mine?"

164

Arianna nodded. "He's your son. There were so many times I thought you'd realize it, but—"

"But," he said, turning to her, his voice sharp, "when I asked you, is the child mine, you said he wasn't."

"No. I mean, yes, that's what I said, but—"

"Another 'but.' You are filled with 'buts,' Arianna. But it must have been an accident. But you slept with no one else. But Gianni is mine." He balled his hands into fists. "But you lied to me when I asked if he was."

Arianna was trembling. She'd seen Dominic angry, but never like this. His face was white, his voice cold, the look in his eyes terrifying. She took a step toward him, held out a hand in supplication but he brushed it aside.

"Try and understand," she pleaded. "I hardly knew you when you asked me if Gianni was yours. I didn't know what you'd do if I admitted that you'd fathered him."

"If I'd *fathered* him?" He came at her quickly; she backed up and he caught her wrist, his fingers pressing hard into her flesh. "You make it sound as if I were a stud horse."

"I didn't mean—"

"You carried my child for nine months, gave birth to him, and never once thought of finding me and telling me I had a son?"

"What for? We were strangers. I didn't think you'd want to know."

"I see. You didn't think I'd want to know, so—"

"Stop repeating everything I say! And let go of my wrist. You're hurting me!"

He looked at his hand, wrapped around hers, as if he'd never seen it before, gave a snort of disgust and flung it from him.

"Four years," he said quietly. "Four long years, during which my son had no father. And now, even though we're married, you still said nothing." His voice rose with barely tempered fury. "Have you an explanation for that, too?"

He saw the muscles in her throat move as she swallowed.

"I—I thought about it on our wedding day."

"You thought about it." Dominic folded his arms. "And you decided...?"

"You know I married you against my will. What did you expect me to do? I was unhappy. I thought I hated you. And—"

"And your unhappiness was more important than the truth."

"No. I didn't say that."

"Oh. Sorry." He smiled politely. "Go on, Arianna. I won't interrupt. This is such a touching story that I'm eager to hear the rest."

"I was angry, and frightened. I didn't know how you'd react." Her eyes brimmed with tears again. "I was afraid you'd try to take my son from me."

"I see. First, I was a stranger who would deny paternity of the child in your womb. Next, I was a crazed monster who'd try and take that child from you. Amazing that I can be both, don't you think?"

Temper flared under Arianna's despair. "Don't talk to me as if I were a fool, Dominic! You're taking two different sets of circumstances and mixing them together."

"In that case, let's skip ahead. Forget our wedding day. Let's consider the weeks that came after it." His mouth thinned. "Six weeks, to be exact. Six weeks during which you could have said at any time, Dominic, I have something to tell you."

"By then, things had grown more complicated." Arianna moistened her lips. "I saw that my son—"

"Our son," Dominic snapped.

"I saw that he'd come to love you. And that you—that you seemed to love him."

"And those are certainly two perfect reasons for not telling the boy and me the truth."

"Our marriage wasn't going well," Arianna said, rushing past the sarcastic words. "I thought it might not last, and—"

"You mean, you hoped it wouldn't last. And if it didn't, why would you ever want me to learn the truth?"

"No," she said quickly, "it wasn't like that. I knew I'd have to tell you, but I thought—I thought—"

"You thought?"

The room was warm with midsummer heat, but Arianna began to shake.

"I thought," she said in a whisper, "more than ever, that you might try and take Jonathan from me. And then you were hurt in the accident, and I knew how I really felt about you, and I knew I had to tell you, but the time was never—was never right."

"That's because you'd gone long past the right time, Arianna. The day you learned you carried my child was the day you should have started searching for me."

"Try to see this from my vantage point," she pleaded. "I thought—"

"I know what you thought. That you could play God. Make my decisions for me. Make my child's decisions for him. Keep us from knowing we were father and son."

Arianna glared at him, eyes bright with defiance. "You make it sound so easy, but what was I supposed to do? Hire a private detective? Ring your doorbell, introduce myself and say, hi, remember me? We spent a couple of hours in bed a couple of months ago and oh, by the way, I'm pregnant."

"That would have been a good start."

"Stop being so damned sanctimonious! Think about how you'd have reacted to that kind of announcement. All those women, eager to marry you for your money, remember what you said? Are you going to tell me you mightn't have thought that's what I was after, too?" She stepped forward, her eyes locked to his. "Be honest, Dominic. What would you have done if I'd come to you five years ago?"

Dominic tried to get past the anger burning hot in his belly while he considered what she'd said.

What *would* he have done? Welcomed her into his life? Rejoiced in the fact that a night of anonymous sex was going to saddle him with at least an eighteen year commitment?

Probably not.

He'd have been upset, angry, disbelieving. He'd have questioned her motives, demanded a DNA test...but, in the end, he'd have done the right thing. Financial support. Visitation rights. A man who grew up without a father wouldn't ignore his own offspring.

But would he have felt the same burst of joy at the news he'd impregnated a woman he'd met at a party as he felt knowing a little boy named Gianni was his? Because he did feel joy, tucked away under all his anger.

The answer was simple.

He would not.

Loving a child you knew was one thing. Loving a handful of cells in the womb of a stranger was another. He was willing to admit that.

The part he couldn't forgive was what had happened in the last six weeks. Arianna wasn't a mystery woman anymore, she was his wife. His wife! She'd had all this time to tell him about Gianni and she hadn't. Was it fear that had kept her quiet...or was it his desire to adopt the boy that had forced her to admit everything?

Her secret would have been uncovered once his lawyers began asking for birth certificates, hospital records, who in hell knew what.

Was that why she'd suddenly told him the truth?

And those words, that declaration of love. False. As false as she was.

He swung away from her, his heart filled with pain.

To think he'd imagined himself in love with her. That he'd prayed she loved him, too. *Dio*, he was pitiful! As easy a mark as the tourists he'd played for suckers when he was a boy.

But he wasn't a boy anymore. He was a man who'd been taken in by a clever woman, and he wasn't helpless. He'd built his fortune on an ability to make quick, intelligent decisions.

It was time to make one now.

His wife was the mother of his son. She was also extraordinary in bed. Two admirable qualities, he thought coldly, and knew what he had to do.

He turned and faced her, watched her search his eyes to discover her fate.

"You're right," he said. "I can take Gianni from you."

"If you try, I'll fight you with everything I have!"

He had to admire her courage. She was white-faced, she was trembling, she had to know he held all the cards...but she was still as fierce as a mother bear guarding her cub.

"We're in Italy. My country. My laws." His smile was razor-sharp. "My connections, and my money. What do you think would be the odds that you'd win?" He let that sink in. When he saw the shadow of fear in her eyes, he spoke again. "But taking you from Gianni would hurt him, and I love my son too much to do that."

Arianna sagged with relief. "I love him too much to hurt him, too," she said quietly. "I know it will be hard, but we can get past this."

"Get past what? The fact that I'm Gianni's father? That you're a liar?" Dominic shook his head. "I don't think so."

"I only lied because I had to. Can't you see that?"

"Oh, I see many things." He came toward her, enjoying the way she edged away. "For instance, I see how wrong I was to think our marriage was based on honesty. But that's all right, *cara*. Without taking you as my wife, I'd never have known I had a son. Gianni would have grown up thinking his father had abandoned him—and I could have passed him on the street someday and not have known he was mine.''

Arianna was weeping openly, the tears streaming down her face. For a heartbeat, Dominic wanted to take her in his arms and tell her—tell her—

Tell her what? She'd lied to him, not just about Gianni but about loving him.

The moment of weakness passed. He'd been a fool before. He damned well would never be one again.

''Never mind, *cara*. I've always been a pragmatist. Maybe that's the reason I have to admit that this has all worked out. I have Gianni. He has me. And he has you, a mother he loves.'' He smiled thinly. ''And, there's something to sweeten the package. Your performance in bed last night.'' Dominic raised his hand to his forehead in a mocking salute. ''My compliments, Arianna. It was as memorable as it was the first time we met.''

Fury replaced the anguish in her eyes. This was the real Dominic Borghese, and she hated him with a passion.

''You're despicable,'' she said, her voice shaking with emotion. ''I don't know why I ever thought anything else.''

''*Cara*, you're not paying attention. I'm trying to tell you that I'm going to keep you.''

''Damn you, don't call me…'' Arianna's mouth dropped open. ''What did you say? You're going to *keep* me?''

Dominic gave a lazy shrug. ''It's the most sensible thing to do. I won't divorce you and take sole custody of my son—and please, don't bother telling me I couldn't do it. I can do anything I set my mind to.'' He spoke softly, but there was no mistaking the steel behind the words. ''Surely you've learned that by now.''

Oh, she had learned everything she needed to know. That he was cruel and vindictive, that he'd stop at nothing to get revenge. It sickened her to think of how she'd lain in his arms last night, how she'd let him use her body, her heart.

"I despise you," she whispered. "You *are* a monster, just as you said. Do you hear me? You're a—"

"I'm a man who sees right through you." His expression hardened. "And I'm warning you, Arianna. Behave yourself, be a good mother to my son and a gifted courtesan in my bed, and I won't throw you out. I'd hate to lose a woman with such assets."

She swung at him and her fist found its mark. It was a good, clean shot to the jaw. He had to admire her for it, and for the defiance shining in her eyes.

"A woman of many talents," he said, and he cupped her nape, dragged her to him and kissed her.

Arianna fought, but even with one arm in a cast, Dominic was far too strong. After a few seconds, she gave up and stood unmoving in his rough embrace.

At last, he raised his head.

"You can hate me all you like," he said thickly, "but when I take you to bed, you'll spread your legs and moan, just as you did last night, or I'm liable to reconsider. Do you understand? Your gifts are varied, but there's a limit to my patience. Gianni can learn to live without you, if he must, and I can always find another playmate."

He let go of her and she stared at him, wondering how she could ever have thought she loved him.

"I hate you. I truly, truly hate you!" Her voice trembled, then rose as he walked away from her. "Do you hear me, Dominic? I hate you!"

She heard his footsteps echoing through the empty rooms, then the sound of the front door slamming shut. After a long time, she wiped her eyes and made her way through the house and down the steps.

The Ferrari was where she'd left it. Dominic was striding along the narrow, tree-lined road. He had his cell phone to his ear and she knew he must be calling his driver to come and pick him up.

She climbed into the car, turned the key and shifted into

gear as soon as the engine roared to life. Foot pressed to the floor, she zoomed past him, shooting a glance in the mirror as she did, smiling with satisfaction when she saw the gray dust blow into his face.

But her smile was only a memory by the next day, after she'd telephoned virtually every attorney in Rome, identified herself as the wife of Dominic Borghese and asked for information on divorce and child custody.

Their advice was always the same.

She could stay in the marriage and keep her son.

Or she could leave it...and lose him.

CHAPTER THIRTEEN

FALL came to Rome and though everyone said the city's climate was milder than New York's, Arianna felt chilled all the time.

She needed to eat more pasta, Rosa said, to warm her bones. She needed to drink more *vino,* Gina said, to thicken her blood. Arianna smiled at each of them and said she was sure she'd get used to the colder weather.

It wasn't true.

It wasn't the weather that chilled her, or a lack of nourishing food or earthy red wine. Her heart was frozen, that was the reason, and nothing would ever thaw it.

She was living with a stranger who despised her. She told herself that was all right. After all, she felt the same way about him.

Gianni, at least, was happy.

"We have to talk about my son," Dominic had said brusquely the day the boy was due back from his visit to the *marchesa.*

"*Our* son," Arianna had said, and he'd acknowledged the correction with a curt nod.

He'd done most of the talking. That was all right, too. Arianna had no wish to drag their child into the mess they'd made. They'd agreed to go on as before, sharing meals, keeping up the pretence that they were a married couple the same as anybody else.

They'd sat Gianni down that same evening and carefully told him Dominic was his father.

Her little boy's eyes had grown wide with wonder.

"My father? You mean, I've got a daddy? Like Bruno?"

"Yes," Dominic had said, taking the boy into his lap. "Just like Bruno."

"Did you 'dopt me?" Gianni asked, looping an arm around Dominic's neck.

Dominic cleared his throat. "I didn't have to. You're my son."

"For real?"

"For real," Dominic replied, with a little smile.

"How come you didn't live with us before? How come nobody told me? How come—"

"It's a long story and we'll tell it to you someday. For now all that matters is that we're together—and we always will be."

Gianni thought that over. "So, you and Mommy made me together?"

"Yes."

"But you only just got married. How could I have been borned before then?"

"Your mother and I knew each other a long time ago, Gianni. Then we—we lost each other."

"Bruno lost a kitten once," Gianni had replied solemnly. "He didn't know where it went, but then his dad found it in the house next door. Did you and Mom lose each other like that?"

"Something like that," Dominic had said, and changed the subject.

Arianna knew Dominic was right. They'd have to tell the boy more someday. For now, the explanation her husband had offered was enough.

Her husband, she thought, as she sat on the terrace wrapped in a heavy sweater. The man she loathed.

Her son worshipped him.

Why wouldn't he? Not a night went by that Dominic didn't come home with some special treat. He was buying the child's affection, stealing it from her....

Except, he wasn't.

Gianni offered his love freely, and how could she blame him? Dominic hated her, but he loved his son. And he was a great father, warm and loving, consistent in setting down simple but meaningful rules. He played with Gianni every evening after dinner, took him places on the weekends.

Her husband was the best father a child could have.

And she—she was turning into the kind of mother a child didn't deserve.

She was listless. Unenthusiastic. Dull. Worst of all, she was weepy. Oh, she never broke down in front of Gianni. As bad as things might be, she'd never let that happen. She saved her tears for the darkness of night, when she lay alone in the guest room bed, waiting—as she had in the past—for her husband to come and claim her.

"Signora?"

Arianna turned toward the door. "Yes, Rosa?"

"I wondered…do you prefer chicken or fish this evening?"

Rosa had taken to asking her questions she'd never bothered asking before. Arianna suspected it was deliberate, an act of kindness meant to draw her into some kind of participation in life. What must the woman think of a bride who spent her days moping?

"Signora?"

"Fish," Arianna said, for the housekeeper's sake. "Fish sounds fine."

"And for a vegetable? I bought some—"

"You decide."

Rosa's face fell. "As you wish," she said, and her sigh seemed to linger even after she stepped back inside.

Arianna rose from her chair and walked slowly to the terrace railing.

Even Gina sensed something was wrong. She'd gone back to issuing polite invitations to coffee. Arianna had accepted a couple of them, hoping they'd cheer her up, but it hadn't worked.

She moped by day and hated herself for it.

And she waited by night, and hated herself even more.

Dominic had made such ugly threats that day at the villa. She'd been steeled for his appearance in her room that same night.

She should have known better.

Her husband wouldn't take her by force. She'd called him a monster, but he wasn't. He was just a man, as vulnerable as any other. More vulnerable, maybe. Life had scarred him and without intending to, she'd managed to open the old wounds.

She'd hurt him deeply, and he'd retaliated. He'd been in a blind rage when he'd told her what he'd do to her. She should have known it was an empty threat.

Dominic wouldn't force himself on her. In her heart, she'd know that all along. But if he did come to her as she lay dreaming of how it could have been if he'd loved her, if he drew back the blankets, touched her with his gentle hands, kissed her with tenderness and then with passion, whispered the words she longed, oh longed to hear…

Arianna blinked back her tears.

He wouldn't. His pride wouldn't permit it. He would never forgive her.

She'd never forgive him, either. Never. She had feelings, too, and he'd trampled them to dust. She would hate him for the rest of her life.

A cold wind moaned through the denuded garden in the courtyard below. Arianna felt the wind's bitter touch, bowed her head and wept.

Dominic scanned the last page of the document lying on his desk, picked up his pen and scrawled his signature at the bottom.

Done, at last. The Silk Butterfly belonged to Arianna.

He'd meant to sign it over weeks before, but first there'd been the car accident and then…

And then, he'd been too blind with fury to think straight.

He was much calmer now. All his anger had drained away. What was the sense in it? He had gained a son. It wasn't as if he'd lost a wife.

He'd never had one in the first place.

Dominic pushed back his chair, swiveled it around and stared out the window at the ruins of the Coliseum. It was one hell of a view and more than a couple of major hotel chains had tried to buy it from him, but he always refused to sell.

There was something about the sight of that ancient building that reached right inside him. He used to imagine it as it had once been, filled with noise and energy, gladiators facing whatever life tossed at them with courage and pride.

His perspective had changed. Lately, the sight was a constant reminder that no matter how hard a man tried, life could always find a way to defeat him.

Almost always, Dominic thought, and turned his chair around.

"Celia?" he said, stabbing the button on his intercom. "Celia? Dammit, don't you hear me?"

"The entire city can hear you," his assistant said calmly, "without the intercom."

Dominic jerked his head up. Celia stood in the doorway, the usual portrait of efficiency, pen and notebook in hand. He glowered but decided to ignore the comment.

"Did you make those phone calls?"

"I did."

"And? Must I pull each word from you?"

"And, only one of the shops has heard of the new toy."

"I don't care how many have or haven't heard of it. What I want to know is—"

"If I found one in stock. Yes. Felici's had a Kitty Kat Robot. It will be wrapped and ready for you to pick up."

"Good." Dominic got to his feet. "I'm leaving."

"So I see." Celia watched her boss walk past her toward the reception desk, her expression as dispassionate as ever. Her boss was not a happy man. She couldn't understand it. He had a beautiful wife and a child he obviously loved, but it wasn't enough. There were times she wanted to shake him…but there were certain liberties even she would not take.

She sighed, stepped behind his desk to straighten it for the next day, spotted the document lying there and scanned it so she could file it away…

"Signore Borghese? *Signore!*" He turned as she hurried after him. "You forgot this."

"Ah. *Grazie.* I'm glad you noticed."

"Oh, I am, too. A man who brings gifts to his wife and child may be able to buy happiness, sooner or later."

Dominic's face reddened. "What did you say?"

Celia stood tall. "Go ahead. Fire me. What you do with your life isn't my business."

"No," he said coldly, "it is not. Watch yourself, Celia. Some day, you'll go too far."

"Your son worships you. Your wife adores you. And still you march around here with a face that terrifies your employees and drives away your clients."

"That's nonsense. And I know my son loves me. You don't have to point it out."

"Your wife does, too."

"That's it. Get your things together. You're fired."

"Fire me. It won't change the facts."

"Dammit," Dominic roared, punching his fist against the wall, "how dare you tell me what my wife feels?"

"She lived in that hospital when you were hurt. She never left your side. She thought you were dying, *signore,* and if that had happened, I think she would have died, too."

"You don't know what you're talking about."

"Don't I?" Celia smiled sadly. "*Buona notte, signore.* I'll pack my things."

"Don't pack anything," Dominic growled. "Who would employ you, except me? Keep your job, keep your tongue and trust me when I tell you that you don't know everything."

"Trust has to be earned, Signore Borghese. It isn't a commodity you can demand of a person."

"Riddles. Just what I need. What in hell is that supposed to mean?"

"Only that *you* don't know everything, either, especially when it comes to the feelings of women. Good night, *signore.*"

Dominic opened his mouth, then shut it. Could a man ever win an argument like this? How could you discuss feelings? It was as he'd explained to Arianna, that day at the villa. Men knew feelings existed, but facts were what mattered.

Only facts.

Grim-faced, he left the building, climbed into his car and set off for the toy store, Kitty Kat Robot, and another evening of trying to figure out why he should give a damn about his dead marriage when he didn't love his wife.

When she, heaven knew, didn't love him.

Gianni climbed into his bed with his Kitty Kat clutched to his chest.

"Thank you again for my present, Daddy."

Dominic's heart still swelled at that word on his son's lips.

"You're welcome, Gianni." He bent down and kissed the boy's forehead. "Sleep well, son."

"I will, unless I hear Mommy crying."

"Unless... What do you mean?"

"Mommy cries sometimes. Late at night. It's just a tiny

little sound, like Kitty Kat made when we turned the switch on and she went 'meow,' remember?"

Dominic swallowed hard. "Maybe it isn't your mommy. It could be a sound from outside."

"Mommy said the same thing when I asked her about it, but I know it's her." Gianni hesitated. "Daddy? 'Member when I asked you why you and Mom didn't sleep in the same room? An' you said husbands and wives didn't always do that?"

Dominic nodded. "I remember."

"Mommies and daddies do. I asked Bruno. He told me."

Bruno. A four-year-old boy supplying answers to questions a thirty-four-year-old man couldn't answer.

"Not always."

"Maybe if you and Mom were in the same room, she wouldn't cry."

Dio, Dominic thought, and pulled the blanket to his son's chin.

"Go to sleep, Gianni."

"Buona notte, Papa."

Dominic smiled. "Good night, *mio figlio.*"

He shut off the light, closed the door and stood silently in the hall. Now what? His wife wept because he wouldn't let her leave him, his secretary was convinced that he was a fool, and his son thought the answer to everything was sharing a room.

Maybe it was.

Maybe what he needed, what they both needed, was to go to bed together. That was what he'd warned her would happen. He could still do it. Walk into Arianna's bedroom tonight, pull down the blankets, strip off her nightgown...

Dominic leaned his forehead against the wall.

Making love to a woman who hated him wasn't the answer. Perhaps giving her the Butterfly was. Then she'd have the son she adored and the shop she loved.

Maybe that would be enough to make her smile again.

He took a deep breath and walked into the sitting room. It was empty. Of course. Arianna left it as soon as Gianni went to bed. He paused, inhaling the light fragrance of her perfume, remembering how it had scented her skin the night they'd made love. No. He wouldn't think about that. Love had nothing to do with what they'd shared.

Why sentimentalize sex?

The paper giving her the Butterfly was in the pocket of his suit jacket. He retrieved it, smoothed out the creases, went down the hall to her room and knocked.

"Yes?"

"It's me." *Brilliant, Borghese. Who else would it be?* "I, uh, I need to talk to you."

"Can't it wait until morning?"

"No," he said tightly, "it cannot."

There was silence. He thought he heard the faint rustle of fabric. Then the lock turned. He tried not to focus on the fact that her door was locked against him. It would only spark his anger, and he wasn't going to lose control like that again.

The door opened a couple of inches. Arianna peered out at him. Her face was shiny, her hair was brushed out so it hung loose to her shoulders, she was wearing a simple white terry cloth robe, and he knew, in that instant, that he wasn't just a fool, he was a deceitful fool because he'd never stopped loving his wife.

"May I come in?"

She moved back. He stepped inside the room.

"What do you want, Dominic? It's late, and—"

"It's eight o'clock. *Dio,* don't look at me like that. I'm not going to—"

Never stopped loving her, and never would stop loving her.

"—not going to touch you."

"Tell me what you want, please."

He thrust the paper at her. "Here."

She looked at it, her hair falling forward against her cheeks. How he longed to smooth back the soft curls, slide his fingers into it and raise her face to his.

She looked up, frowning in puzzlement. "What is this?"

"It's what I promised you. Ownership of the Butterfly."

"Oh. Thank you."

She tossed the paper aside. He looked at it, then at her.

"Oh? That's it?"

"What did you expect me to say? Good night, Dominic."

She opened the door wider so that he'd get the idea. Well, he got it. But he wasn't going anywhere until she explained herself.

"Did you actually read that document? Do you know what it is? I said that I've turned over the—"

"I heard what you said. Good night."

"Wait a minute." A muscle jumped in his jaw. "That's what this was all about, remember? The Butterfly. I said I'd give it to you if you married me."

"My grandmother will be happy. Thank you again. And good—"

"Dammit, Arianna, what do you want from me? I kept our bargain and all you can say is—"

"What do you want me to say?" Her eyes flashed; he looked at her in surprise as it occurred to him that he hadn't seen that look, that anger and vitality, on her face in a very long time. "I thanked you. End of story."

"The hell it is!"

"Keep your voice down. You'll wake Gianni."

Dominic kicked the door shut behind him. "You'll wake him anyway. He says he hears you crying during the night."

Color flooded her face. "I do not cry! Whatever Gianni hears, it's not me weeping."

"Of course not. Why would you weep?"

"Indeed." She folded her arms, lifted her chin. "Why would I?"

"I don't know." Dominic moved toward her. She retreated. He was angry already and that made him angrier. What was she afraid of? Had he ever hurt her? Had he ever stormed in here and taken her, as he'd threatened to do? As he'd ached to do, all these weeks—except he didn't want to take her in anger. He wanted her to come to him willingly, to sigh his name as she had once done, to kiss him and tell him, with each kiss, that she loved him as much as he loved her.

"Do you weep because you think you must tolerate my presence in your life?" He clasped her shoulders. "Because you have to look at my face each morning and know that I am your husband? Is that the reason you cry, Arianna?"

She shook her head. Tears glittered on her lashes, then spilled down her cheeks.

"Answer me, dammit." He shook her. "Do you weep because you hate me?"

"I weep because I love you!" The words burst from her throat. She knew she was making a mistake, that he'd never believe her, that she was making herself even more vulnerable, but she couldn't hide what she felt anymore, not from him, not from herself. "I love you, Dominic. I know you don't want to hear it, but—"

She cried out as his mouth crushed hers in a kiss so filled with passion it made her dizzy.

"*Cara mia. Il mio cuore,*" he whispered, "you are my heart. My soul."

"Dominic. Dominic, my love…"

He kissed her again, cupped her face, scattered more kisses on her eyelids, her nose, her cheeks.

"I've been so cruel, *cara.* But when I thought you'd deceived me…"

"I know it was wrong. I should have told you about

Gianni as soon as we were married, but I was afraid. I didn't know you, didn't know what you'd do—"

"*Si*. I understand. You were cautious, and you were right to be. You had a child you were determined to protect at all costs." Dominic took a deep breath and lifted her face to his. "I let the ghosts of my past rule my heart, Arianna. I wanted you to love me and when I thought you didn't... I was wrong to lash out at you, *cara*. Can you forgive me?"

"There's nothing to forgive. I hurt you. I didn't meant to, but I did." Arianna framed his face with her hands, brought his lips to hers and kissed him. "I'll never hurt you again, *il mio amore*. I swear it."

Dominic gathered her tightly in his arms. "*Ti amo, mia moglie.*"

Such glorious words. Arianna's lips curved in a smile. "And I love you, my husband. I always will."

Dominic lifted his wife in his arms. She linked her hands behind his neck.

"Where are we going?" she said softly.

"To our bedroom. I'm going to make love to my wife." He grinned. "And tomorrow—"

"Just like a man, already planning ahead." She kissed his mouth tenderly. "What about tomorrow?"

"Tomorrow, we'll take Gianni and drive to the villa. It's time our son had a real cat. And a dog. And a pony. And—"

"And a mother and father who love each other," Arianna whispered.

"And who always will," Dominic whispered back, as he carried the woman he loved into his room, and into his life.

Gianni took all the credit for his parents' wedding in the spring.

He and Bruno—"the font of knowledge," Dominic said, laughing—had been discussing things. Bruno said brides always wore white gowns and grooms always wore funny black suits.

Gianni said it wasn't true. He'd been at his parents' wedding and they hadn't dressed that way.

"Well," said Bruno, "they should have."

Gianni mentioned it to his mother. His mother smiled and mentioned it to his father who laughed, hoisted him into the air and said he thought that was a great idea.

Next thing he knew, there was a thing called a bower set up in the garden behind the big house they all lived in now, and it was covered with pink and white roses.

There was a guy playing a violin. A couple of guys, actually. There were guests smiling at each other, and there was good stuff to eat and bubbly stuff to drink and, just like that first time, he even got to taste some.

But this wedding was lots better.

His mom looked like a princess in a long white dress with a big skirt and a neckline that showed her shoulders. She said the dress was made of lace. She had flowers in her hair, like the ones on the bower.

His dad wore a funny black suit, just like Bruno had said, but it didn't look funny on his dad. It looked sort of cool.

He stood next to his dad, under the bower, in a suit that was kind of the same, holding his dad's hand tight as his great-grandma came down the aisle with his mom.

"*Mia bambina,*" he heard his *nonna* whisper, which was silly 'cause his mom wasn't a little girl anymore.

His mom took a step toward his dad, who was looking at her, and—wow! Were those tears in his dad's eyes? There were definitely tears in his mom's.

"*Mia principessa,*" his dad said to his mom, "*come sei bella.*" That was okay because it was true. She really did look like a beautiful princess.

All of a sudden, his *nonna* tapped that black stick of hers against the ground. Everybody seemed surprised. Not him.

His great-grandma was always doing stuff nobody expected. It was one of the bestest things about her.

"You will excuse me, *per favore*," she said, "but I have something of importance to say. Today, the del Vecchios and the Borgheses become one." Then she smiled, in the way that meant she was feeling pretty pleased with herself. "And I am delighted to tell you all that it is good to know an old woman like me can still devise a clever plan that works well, from start to finish."

His mom blinked. So did his dad. Then they began to laugh. Things got quiet after that and the ceremony began, and his great-grandma took his hand and the two of them got a little teary-eyed together.

And when the ceremony was over, and he squeezed between his parents and they lifted him in their arms and they all kissed and hugged each other, Gianni Cabot del Vecchio Borghese figured he was absolutely the luckiest, happiest kid in Italy, in America, in the whole, wide world.

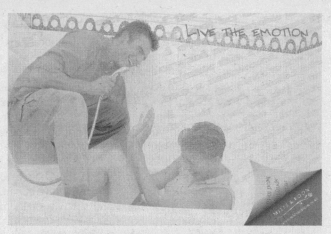

Modern Romance™
...seduction and
passion guaranteed

Tender Romance™
...love affairs that
last a lifetime

Medical Romance™
...medical drama
on the pulse

Historical Romance™
...rich, vivid and
passionate

Sensual Romance™
...sassy, sexy and
seductive

Blaze Romance™
...the temperature's
rising

27 new titles every month.

Live the emotion

MILLS & BOON®

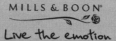

MILLS & BOON

STEPHANIE LAURENS

A Season for Marriage

Available from 18th July 2003

*Available at most branches of WH Smith,
Tesco, Martins, Borders, Eason, Sainsbury's
and all good paperback bookshops.*

0703/135/MB67

9526 JC77

4 FREE

books and a surprise gift!

We would like to take this opportunity to thank you for reading this Mills & Boon® book by offering you the chance to take FOUR more specially selected titles from the Modern Romance™ series absolutely FREE! We're also making this offer to introduce you to the benefits of the Reader Service™—

- ★ FREE home delivery
- ★ FREE gifts and competitions
- ★ FREE monthly Newsletter
- ★ Exclusive Reader Service discount
- ★ Books available before they're in the shops

Accepting these FREE books and gift places you under no obligation to buy, you may cancel at any time, even after receiving your free shipment. Simply complete your details below and return the entire page to the address below. *You don't even need a stamp!*

YES! Please send me 4 free Modern Romance books and a surprise gift. I understand that unless you hear from me, I will receive 6 superb new titles every month for just £2.60 each, postage and packing free. I am under no obligation to purchase any books and may cancel my subscription at any time. The free books and gift will be mine to keep in any case.

P3ZEE

Ms/Mrs/Miss/Mr ....Initials...................................
BLOCK CAPITALS PLEASE

Surname ....

Address ....

....

....Postcode...............................

Send this whole page to:
UK: FREEPOST CN81, Croydon, CR9 3WZ
EIRE: PO Box 4546, Kilcock, County Kildare (stamp required)